Colliding Heavens

Also by

Ellen Ashford

WHO IS THE JOKER IN BID WHIST

COLLIDING

HEAVENS

ELLEN ASHFORD

Denice,

Thank you for
your support!

ASHFORD'S PUBLISHING

Ellen Ashford

COLLIDING HEAVENS

ISBN: 0-9769901-2-1

Books may be ordered from Ashford's Publishing at www.ellenashford.com.

Cover by Ralph Ashford
Manuscript assistant and editor: Jane Haradine

Printed in the United States of America

Afternoon farmers (lazy farmers) will not have a good crop.
Ancient Proverb

A good farmer will plant, cultivate, and harvest
at the right time of day and season.

This book is dedicated to those people who supported me with the last book. To all those who went out and purchased *Who Is the Joker in Bid Whist* and told others about the book, I would like to thank you.

In addition, since the last book, some of the people I care about the most lost their fight with life. They are my brother Horace D. Ashford, his son (my nephew) Horatio B. Ashford, my niece Cassidy Terrielle Jeter who was only six when she was mauled by pit bulls. I also want to say good-bye to William Crosby and so many others who are gone but not forgotten.

On a lighter side of life, I also dedicate this book to Argie Holliman Chibuzo, who has been a good friend.

Acknowledgments

It is a Blessing to have had so many people who were instrumental in helping with the success of *Colliding Heavens*. There are so many different characters in this body of work. Because of cultural differences, I went to the sources for an accurate depiction.

First, I would like to thank Thomas Burrell, president of the Black Farmers and Agriculturalists Association. To Karen Henry, who gave me information about Arab life, I say thank you for helping me with the meaning of names. I would also like to thank Rabbi Michael A. Schadick. When I went to him with the story idea, he gave me needed information.

I also give special thanks to Ralph Ashford, my brother, for the cover of the book.

Thanks to Christina Gubbins and Jane Haradine for all their help.

Thanks also to Tom Kersin for promoting the book.

To Mrs. Clifton Rhodes, thank you for all you have done.

And special loves go out to Deasia and Jeremiah.

Prologue

April 22

Please forgive me, I'm running for my life. I've got the Knights of Darkness chasing me through the middle of Mississippi, and I've heard them say that they're going to either sacrifice me to their gods once I'm caught or hang me after violating my body. Imagine hearing people discuss how they plan to kill you. It's hideous the various ways people have devised to kill others, physically as well as psychologically.

Oh, I'm sorry. Let me introduce myself. My name is Precious Jennings. Yeah, that's me on the cover of the book. The charcoal drawing was from a time in my life when I thought I had the world at my fingertips. I'm a recovering enabler—I just feel like I've got to help everybody. I have a nice home, a luxurious car, the finest friends money can buy, and a boyfriend for whom women would die. My parents were the pillars of the community. They sheltered me from life and heaped the finest finishing school and private schools on me.

I never should have opened the door in the first place. Why was I offering the Knights of Darkness coffee in my living room? Something, maybe my third eye, told me that something wasn't quite right about them.

Now my sister, Jazzy, is I believe the prettiest woman in the world. She is not only pretty, but she's smart as well. But please, I do digress.

I never knew that a group like the Knights of Darkness ever existed. I really never experienced hatred of that magnitude before. It was a trip seeing them in white and black faces, looking like zombies, dressed in black and dancing around an open fire discussing their love for hatred.

You know people say that your life flashes in front of you at death? Well, my life is flashing reds, oranges, and purples irregularly as a car is approaching me from behind. Can you believe that I'm actually out-running a car? I can't feel my heart beating. If my feet are touching the dirt road, I can't feel them doing so. I feel like I'm flying. Yet the car behind me is getting closer to me.

The flashes are more like a blazing fire now, and I really need to concentrate on a strategy that is going to keep me alive, but my life keeps flashing, and I wonder where it all went wrong.

I need to go back some and explain how I got to this point.

I think a really good place to start is at the funeral.

Chapter 1

April 1

The rain is beating down in the hot, overcrowded church as Precious walks hand in hand with her sister, Jazzy, as they march down the long aisle. People stand as they come into the room. The choir sings "Nearer My God to Thee." As the people stand for the family as they parade down the aisle, Precious gazes behind her and notices that the family procession is enormously long—the line goes down the stairs, out the door, and circles the large church. She takes a seat next to her sister while trying to portray a strong façade. She looks around the room for her boyfriend, but doesn't see him anywhere.

There lying in the pink floral casket is her mother, Sarah Jennings. Her mother, who was a strong woman, buried her husband a week ago. Precious's mother died in the same seat that Precious is now sitting in. For a quick second, Precious wonders if the same incident might happen again with her sitting there. These two weeks have been unbearable for Precious, and if Jazzy hadn't been there, Precious doesn't believe she could have survived the two deaths. She recalls the brown casket that sat in the same spot only a week ago, which held the remains of her father. He was a good father and brilliant businessman who would help any child who was in need of either money or proper instruction. Her mother, on the other hand, cared mostly about her two children and sent her two daughters to Pinnacle Finishing School, then to Harvard for Precious and Yale for Jazzy. Mrs. Jennings also had a love for the other children in her family.

Drinking Scott is sitting with the mothers of the church. He looks as though he has consumed a gallon of liquor before coming. He was there last week when their father passed away and is in the same condition he was then. Precious holds her breath, hoping he doesn't cause another commotion. Too late. Drinking Scott starts down toward the casket.

Last week, Precious started to stop him, but her mother told her to leave him alone because Precious had no idea of the loss this man felt for her father. After asking around, Precious finds out that her father had saved Drinking Scott's life by buying a house for him and his family to live in after Drinking Scott lost his job. Precious is sure that there is more to the story, but she hasn't had a chance to research the relationship.

Sarah Jennings' casket has not been closed yet, and Drinking Scott goes over and falls out on the floor in front of it. The ushers gaze at Precious for instructions on this matter, and Precious waves them away, letting them know that she is accepting his behavior. Several minutes later, he staggers off the floor and walks over to Precious and Jazzy and hugs them. His clothes smell as if they haven't been washed in months. Precious knows that his getting up and walking over to the casket will occur at least three times during the eulogy.

The members of the choir begin singing "Trouble Don't Last Always." Jazzy turns to Precious, her older sister, and whispers, "I need a fan and Kleenex. How come you didn't remind me?" An usher hears the comment and quickly places a fan and a box of tissue into Jazzy's lap. Another usher places a chair in the aisle and starts fanning both Precious and Jazzy.

Sarah and Harrison Jennings had been married over fifty years, and the marriage had produced two beautiful, intelligent women. Jessica, known by everyone in the community as Jazzy, wraps her arm around her big sister, who is only one year older than her thirty-four years, and kisses her while pretending to be interested in the service.

Precious remembers how painful it was to tell her mother that their father had had a heart attack on his way home from work, and that he had died in the hospital minutes before Sarah Jennings had had a chance to say good-bye to him. Precious and Jazzy had to make the funeral arrangements because their mother was too distraught about not having said good-bye to him. He hadn't been sick, but two weeks earlier, he had started to complain about chest pains.

Precious is going to miss her mother. The family has a special love for one another. Precious gazes toward her sister, who will be making a speech in several minutes, and wonders if she will be able to make it through it.

Sarah and Harrison had an everlasting love affair. Harrison included Sarah in every part of his life. They often left the two children with relatives as they traveled around the world together, searching out new and interesting places. Harrison owned several supermarkets in the inner city, and those people who couldn't afford to pay, he usually worked out some deal with them that was beneficial to all parties concerned.

Sarah worked as a nurse and usually on her days off she was at the supermarket ordering food and balancing Harrison's books.

Most of the small businesses in the area had had several robberies every year, but the neighbors were always supporting and looking out for the family-owned business as they ran the only supermarkets in the inner city.

Hundreds of people hug Precious and Jazzy and tell them how sorry they are about the deaths of their parents. Some of the people are truly concerned about the sisters and wonder how the two unmarried women will survive their parents' deaths.

Finally the minister, Reverend Lamont, walks up to the podium and looks out over the congregation. He and the Jenningses were really good friends, and the anguish is showing on his face as he starts to read several Bible verses.

Another song from Jazzy's best friends sends several women running up and down the aisle, yet Precious and Jazzy say nothing.

Drinking Scott strolls out another time, drops to the floor, lies there several minutes, and gets up. Precious thinks, *This is too much. I just want to go home and hide in Mom and Dad's closet.* As a child she would go in their bedroom and sit in the closet and sniff the clean clothes that smelled so much like the two of them. She felt secure. Now all her security is gone, and what is left is sure to be confusion.

Precious remembers that after all the funeral arrangements were made for her father that her mother insisted on seeing him alone. Precious waited impatiently outside, wondering about the conversation her mother was having with her dead husband. Precious made a mental note to ask what she said to him. Precious asked her mother, "Why did you want that time with him alone?"

Sarah Jennings told Precious, "I thanked him for the fifty years that he gave me. I thanked him for the two children and the wonderful life he provided for me. I also thanked him for protecting me from other people, and sometimes he protected me from myself." She smiled at Precious, and that was the last time that Precious ever saw her mother smile.

During the home-going celebration, Precious wonders if her parents are together again and, if so, what they are doing at that very moment. She also wonders what heaven is like and if they might be happier there.

Precious twists and turns. She isn't able to find the right seating position.

Mrs. Margaret, who has the largest bosom in town, comes over and gives Precious a hug, and for several seconds Precious gasps for air.

This past week Precious has been exhausted and decides mentally to take a vacation once she has all the family's affairs in order. The ordeal of calling family, making the final funeral arrangements, and collecting insurance policies has been an additional drain on her. She glances at the people around her, all relatives, yet Precious feels so alone. It all seems like a movie to her. She glances around the room one more time for Larry, her boyfriend, and feels betrayed by his not being there.

The choir starts to sing when her cousin Dora squeezes between Precious and Jazzy with a box of tissues.

"I knew after all your organizing today that you would forget the tissue." Dora hands several to Precious while looking around the room, not noticing the box of tissue Precious already has in her hand.

"Wow, girl, everybody in town turned up to Aunt Sarah's funeral."

Precious still doesn't say anything, while taking the tissues from Dora.

Precious recalls her mother's two sisters and their children. Her mother's sisters had large families, and when Sarah Jennings' older sister died, Sarah took care of the twelve children left behind when Uncle Jake was either working or too busy to take care of them.

Sarah Jennings had her own children in addition to her sister's twelve. Sarah's younger sister had seven children and wasn't much assistance in helping bring up the twelve children left behind.

Precious returns to reality when her younger sister gets up to speak.

Jazzy is beautiful as she mounts the stairs. Her dress is short and tight. Her hair flows in every direction as she passes by a gigantic fan in the front of the church. The rain seemed to stop as soon as Jazzy got up. The air-conditioning has gone out in the church and, with all the body heat, Precious thinks that it is too hot for the funeral. Jazzy's long legs are beautiful as she graciously positions herself at the microphone as though she is about to sing a sad blues song. She tosses her hair back as she fumbles with the paper she is about to read.

Her friends know Jazzy as the party starter. She makes everyone around her feel comfortable. She is an anchorperson at WSOL television station. As she starts to speak, she plays with her long hair. Precious knows that Jazzy is doing this because she is nervous. Other people have judged Jazzy as being caught up in the moment of herself. Jazzy doesn't care because she has self-confidence and is always trying to read the latest news while getting her nails done or caring for her real, long-flowing hair, which always seems to be a priority for her.

Carolyn, Precious's malicious cousin, pretends to comfort Precious from the seat behind her and whispers, "Why does Jazzy have ta upstage everything?"

Precious thinks, *Here comes the confusion.*

Dora turns to her younger sister and says, "Why don't you be quiet?"

Carolyn sits back in her pew. Both Precious and Dora know that this isn't the end of her comments or her performance. After Sarah Jennings' heart attack, Carolyn had not bothered to stop by, and this has secretly infuriated Precious. Sarah had gone to all Carolyn's high school plays and spent hours at night comforting Carolyn after her mother passed away, yet Carolyn had no time for the family.

Jazzy continues to speak, her chest out and very poised. Sarah Jennings had paid a great deal of money to send both Precious and Jazzy to finishing school. Those lessons had worked out better for Jazzy than Precious. Jazzy always stands up straight, with her chest out, and looks into the eyes of the person she is talking to, making them feel as though they are the most important person in the world.

Precious smiles and nods, giving her younger sister support as she speaks. Precious remembers the turbulent relationship between Jazzy and their mother. Precious thinks, *They were so much alike.*

Precious remembers the time that her mother had cooked all of Jazzy's favorite foods—meatloaf, mashed potatoes, green beans, home-made rolls, sweet potato pie, and lemonade. Everyone in the big family was about to sit down to eat when there was an argument that erupted in the kitchen between Jazzy and her mother.

Jazzy turned and left the house angry.

Sarah said to her husband, Harrison, as Jazzy left, "Look at that silly girl leaving. At least she could have waited to have the argument after she had dinner." Precious and all her cousins laughed as Jazzy angrily walked to her Porsche.

Later Jazzy told Precious while sitting in Jazzy's beautiful uptown apartment, drinking an expensive bottle of wine, that she had made a big mistake leaving before she had had her meal.

Although Jazzy had not mastered the relationship between mother and daughter, she was very good to her mother, buying her expensive clothes and sending her mother and father on trips around the world. If Jazzy had a million dollars, she would spend half the money on herself and the other half on her mother and father.

Jazzy is very good at her job at WSOL. Awards line her mantel from the Associated Press and other major news organizations. For two straight years, Jazzy has received top honors as an investigative reporter.

Precious remembers the investigative reporting Jazzy did uncovering a construction contract that was earmarked for a minority contractor. She found out that the contractor was actually one of the larger contractors in the city who hired a Black man as the subcontractor and gave the business a different name. Jazzy received death threats and seriously thought about exposing the death threats on her weekly show. There was one thing that she had learned from her parents: Never walk away from a good fight, especially when you know that you're right. Even though her life had been threatened, Jazzy could take care of herself. Not many people knew that she had a black belt in karate and that she had gone to Asia to practice with some of the best professionals in the world. This is a secret between only Jazzy and Precious—this was not known even by their mother.

While Jazzy continues to talk, Precious reflects on what seemed like bad times for her and her mother, which were actually good times in disguise. She remembers the time her mother pulled her aside while she was trying to introduce her mother to some of her more condescending friends at a party that Precious was hosting.

Precious's mother had said, "I'm going home. These people are living in a different galaxy. I can't believe that I gave up my game shows to come to this pompous affair. You ain't even got any real food. I'm going home to cook. If these pretentious wannabes want some real food, come on over to my house, but tell them I have a box right outside my front door. They can deposit their attitudes there and pick them up when they leave my house."

Precious had been embarrassed about how her mother reacted to her first professional party, but for some reason it seemed so funny to her now. Precious forgets that people are around her as she laughs out loud.

Dora whispers, "Girl, are you losing your mind?" Precious just smiles. Relatives sitting around her are confused.

When Jazzy finishes speaking, she comes out of the choir stand slowly and walks toward her big sister and sits next to her.

"How did I do?"

Precious sits close to her and says, "I am so proud of you." Precious has not heard a word she said.

As the casket closes, Carolyn, who is sitting behind Precious, starts to scream loudly and runs up to the casket, crying, "Lord, please take me. Don't take my Auntie Sarah. Lord Jesus … Lord Jesus."

Dora whispers to Precious, "Well, who's going to get up and get that fool?"

Precious whispers back, "I ain't."

Drinking Scott saunters back to the casket and falls one last time.

The ushers from the back of the church swiftly move toward the front. They hadn't expected anything like this at Mrs. Jennings' funeral as Carolyn tries to pull Mrs. Jennings out of the casket, and Drinking Scott pounds his fist on the floor as the ushers try to help him up.

Several ushers crowd around Carolyn to help her regain control of her emotions. Precious, Jazzy, and Dora watch in disbelief.

Even though Precious knows that the people around her mean well, she also remembers that her mother did not like half of them, and the other half she tolerated. But Sarah truly loved her children and her nieces and nephews.

She tries to remember the words her mother spoke to her right before her father's funeral. Precious remembers her mother saying, "Why don't you find a man that's gonna love you?"

Precious tried to explain to her mother that it was the most difficult task she had ever had to encounter, but that she would keep trying to find a man who would love her unconditionally the way others in the family had.

After the funeral service, Precious wants to go back to the home that she has grown up in. While Jazzy entertains family and friends in the church's basement, Precious excuses herself, stating that she hasn't had much sleep since the passing of her parents.

The rooms in her parents' home are both silent and cold, even though it is one of the warmest days in the year. She calls an airline to purchase a ticket that will take her as far away as she can go. She decides to travel to the south of France.

After hanging up the phone, she sits on the couch, wondering what to do next, when she hears sounds in her mother's old room. Precious grabs her purse and is ready to leave when she hears someone walking toward her. Precious makes her way to the front door but then hears a familiar sound. She turns around, and there stands her mother. Precious hasn't had any sleep for weeks, and the illusion seems real to her.

Precious gasps for air, then falls to the floor. Her mother just stands there. "Well you might as well get up. I came back to help you."

When Precious recovers, she runs to the kitchen and pours a glass of water from the pitcher in the refrigerator. She takes a sip and wonders if her mind is playing tricks on her. She takes another sip, then turns around. There is her mother still standing there. "Like I said, I'm here to help you find your way."

Mrs. Jennings walks through the kitchen into the living room and slides her fingers across the surface of the grand piano, checking for dust. Then she says, "What happened to Kevin?"

"He was too fat."

"David?"

"Too stuck up."

"Richard?"

"Too poor."

"Carl?"

"He didn't grow up."

"George?"

"He likes other men."

"Morris?"

"He two-timed me."

"Terrance?"

"Too many drugs."

"Michael?"

"He needed some drugs."

"Let's see … Coolio?"

"Pimpin'."

"Marvin?"

"Doesn't love anyone but himself."

"Nick?"

"He likes White women."

"Jerome?"

"Gangster."

"Tim?"

"His name is Kim now."

"Shoot, girl, you can find more things wrong with people. That's probably why you don't have any friends. You're so picky."

"Mom, come on. These are some major flaws."

"Your dad had flaws, too, and I managed to help him develop into the man that he was."

"Mom, this ain't the good old days. You can go out with the wrong guy and end up dead."

"There are going to be people that you'll come in contact with, and you will listen to them, and you may learn more about life."

The doorbell rings, and Precious turns quickly, gladly averting her attention to the new challenge standing behind the ringing of a bell. She walks swiftly to the door, refusing to check the peephole before flinging the door open.

There stand three women with whom she works at the DeVeux Advertising Agency, one of the largest advertising firms in the Midwest.

All three women have on either Ralph Lauren or Liz Claiborne suits, and they are elegantly dressed in their Gucci shoes and purses.

Trina walks around Precious's mother's house with her elbow and hand up as the expensive purse hangs from her arm, showing her neatly manicured nails.

Sheena looks at the barstool close to the kitchen where she gracefully hoists herself up, raising her hemline past her knee. She lights a cigarette. Directing her question to Precious, she asks, "So do you have any wine?"

Precious starts to answer when the third woman, Mona, checks the room for an advantageous place to sit. She finally decides on Mrs. Jennings' favorite chair. She starts the vibrating mechanisms on the side of the chair before she speaks. "Ah, this feels good. Sheena, if you wanted wine, you should have brought some. You know she just buried her mama today. Precious, can I have this chair?"

Precious wonders why these women are visiting her today. Precious has a million errands to run, and she would much rather talk with her deceased mother than carry on a pretentious conversation with these women who did not even come to her mother's funeral.

Precious thinks, *I ain't seen these heifas since my daddy died. They didn't even send me a damn card. Now they're sitting in my house like we're the best of friends, asking me for liquor, sitting in my mama's favorite chair, acting like they just stepped off the runway in Paris.*

Precious tries to be diplomatic, but after the weeks of planning funerals, she would just rather say what's on her mind.

Precious goes and stands next to the door and says, "Look, y'all, I've got a lot of things I need to do tonight. I don't have time to deal with this. Besides, y'all ain't my friends anyway. Where were you when I really needed you? Where were you when my father died and my mother died? If I could have just gotten a call from you sayin' 'Hang in there,' but I haven't heard from y'all, and now you're over here asking me for something to drink. You didn't even come to my mother's funeral. The three of you are like buzzards coming in for the kill. I would ask you what you want, but I really don't care."

Precious opens the door and sways her hand back and forth for them to leave.

Mona closes the door and directs her remarks to Precious.

"I know you don't like us, and that's cool. We've tried our best to get along with you, inviting you to dinners, asking you out to lunch, and making a special effort to include you at parties where real deals are being made, but you didn't want to go. Who are you to look down your nose at us? We didn't come to the funeral because why go somewhere and be phony."

Mona pushes back her hair, and Precious realizes that the true meaning of the visit is about to be exposed.

Sheena and Trina move next to Mona. Precious senses that Mona has been nominated to deliver the bad news.

Mona clears her throat and says, "You know that atrocious Alexandra Davis McBride account that no one wanted to handle because of that old dragon lady Mrs. McBride? Well, it needs special attention. Someone has to go to Mississippi and kiss up to the wicked witch of the South. None of us have those skills. We had a departmental meeting last week when you were on family leave and decided that you should service the account. For some reason, you have that special Southern charm, so now you get a chance to use it.

"I thought that we could soften the blow by telling you before you came in to work and hear it from someone else. Morse messed up the account by treating her like she was stupid or something. You have to stay down there until she's comfortable with how we're advertising her herbal products and she signs the contract. She told DeVeux himself that if he couldn't find her a courteous representative that she was taking her account to another advertising agency."

Trina reaches for the door and says, "This might be a good time for you to find yourself."

Precious once again opens the door. She will not give them the satisfaction of witnessing the disappointment she is now feeling, nor will she utter any words that they may take back to the corporation to use against her.

Precious just smiles as she says good-bye to them.

"Mother, where are you?"

The house is silent.

Somewhere in Mississippi

"General, you called for me?"

"Yes. Please come in." The General takes a sheet of paper out of his desk and motions for the Sergeant to come closer.

"I want these people. I tried to get them last year, but things didn't work out."

"General, I don't understand."

The General puts his hands over his eyes and rubs them for several seconds, then says, "I want these people kidnapped. They didn't cooperate last year, so I want you to snatch them."

"General, what you are proposing is against the law. We could go to jail if anyone finds out about it."

"Have you forgotten our mission, Sergeant? We promised to cleanse this country. I've tried infiltrating their systems—I sent my grandson to their colleges, and that didn't work. I want to see a change in my lifetime."

The Sergeant scratches his arm. "I don't know if I agree with kidnapping people for a cause, sir."

The General swings around in his chair and stares out the window, "Do you want me to give this assignment to someone else?"

The Sergeant takes a seat close to the desk and contemplates for several minutes before saying, "I'll do it, but this will be my last assignment. I'm quitting after this."

The General is still glaring out the window. "You know, that might be a good idea."

Chapter 2

April 2

The morning after the funeral, Jazzy calls Precious, ecstatic. "Girl, I tried to call you last night. You should have been there at Ryan's house. There was this man there no one knew. He kept trying to get information from us about you. He was tall and good-looking. He said that you dated several years ago. He gave me his telephone number, and he asked me to tell you to give him a call sometime. Ryan didn't like him and finally asked him to leave. Do you know him?"

Precious leans back in her seat. "No, I don't recall anyone like that."

Jazzy says with a smile on her face, "No one is stalking you, are they?"

Precious laughs. "Nope. Girl, I don't have time for this. I might be going to Mississippi for an indefinite period of time." Precious unwraps a box of candy sitting on her nightstand and starts to eat the chocolate with both nuts and cherry filling. She relaxes as her sister continues to talk.

"What are you talking about? I thought you told me when we were making arrangements for Mom that you really wanted to go to the south of France."

Precious is close to tears but is able to pop another piece of chocolate candy into her mouth as if this is going to stop the tears from flowing before she says, "Well now I'm going to the south of Mississippi."

"What happened? How do you know that?"

"Mona's crowd came over here last night and told me what I can expect when I go into work today."

"Precious, you deserve to take some time off. Shit, you haven't had any sleep for over two weeks."

"Jazzy, sister, I've heard some weird things about this town I'm going to."

"What are you talking about?"

"I've heard that something's not right there. I can't remember where I heard about it, but I heard it."

"Before you take your behind down there, you better find out what's going on. I'm not losing my sister too."

"Yeah, I will."

"You're not listening to me, Precious. I told you not to go. You don't have to prove anything to anybody. Find another job."

"Yeah, I will."

"You will do what?"

"I'll research the town before I go."

"Promise me that you won't make a move?"

"I promise that I'll talk to you before I leave."

"Damn, you're so stubborn."

"Jazzy, I've got to go to work for a few hours. I need to contact my clients. I don't want to lose them. I'll do my homework before I make a move."

"Precious, you've got to be crazy. You've been up all night and all day for the last two weeks and now you're going in to work? How are you going to make an informed decision about going to Mississippi when you can't even decide to go to bed at night? If I had known that you were going to do something stupid like going in to work, I would have been over there taking everything you need to go in to work with today—your purse, that expensive attaché case, and your car keys. You must be out of your mind."

Precious tries to reach for her cup of coffee as she continues to talk to her sister.

"I know that you wouldn't have let me go in today. That's why I didn't tell you my plans. I've got to go. I'll call you from my cell phone this afternoon."

"Call me? Sister, Charles surprised me last night. He told me he was taking me away. At first I wasn't impressed, but then he told me that he was taking me to the Bahamas," Jazzy screams in the phone. "I'm leaving in a half an hour. I hate to leave you here alone, but I've got to go. I would ask you to go with us, but I know already that you aren't going. Promise me that you won't make a move? Promise me?"

"I promise you."

"I'll call you from my cell when I get there and have a relaxed minute. Peace."

Jazzy hangs up the phone after having the last word.

Precious feels a little jealous as she hangs up the phone. She thinks, *I've got your peace all right.*

Precious pictures her little sister and the man she is about to marry sitting on the beach while some fine young man brings them pina coladas all day. Precious says softly, "Why can't that be me?"

She picks up the phone to call Larry, then slams it down. She thinks about what makes her even like him. He doesn't call. He wasn't there for her, and he disappears for weeks without a trace.

Precious walks over to her dresser drawer and sticks her hand into a candy bowl with different types of candy. She peels off the wrapper on a mint and pops it into her mouth and just chews until it has dissolved.

Precious washes her hands and takes a caramel-colored suit out of her closet and examines it for stains, even though she has just gotten it back from the cleaners. Precious is meticulous when it comes to her clothes and her home. She is going back to work and still she doesn't feel as though she has thoroughly cleaned her parents' house. Precious is concerned about her level of patience with her supervisors and believes that she is on the verge of snapping. She knows that she is about to snap when things around her are not clean enough for her.

There is also an uneasy feeling about going in to work. She wishes that she could take a full month off and sleep and travel the world.

Precious thinks about her parents' clothes in their closet. This is a job that she would prefer not to do. The more she sits around thinking about the task, the sadder she knows she will become.

Precious thinks, *I'll box up all of Mom's clothes while Jazzy is gone. Jazzy can get what she wants when she returns from her trip, and I'll send everything else to Goodwill. But if I have to go out of town, I could wait until I get back. ... I think I'm going to wait. If those clothes are out of sight, they might be out of mind.*

Precious decides to move all of her belongings from her extravagant condo into her mother's modest inner-city home. The house is paid for, and friendly warm people who attend the same church as her family would surround her.

Precious pushes the caramel suit back into the closet, thinking, *This suit is too festive.*

She searches the closet for another one. She stands in front of the mirror holding a navy blue suit close to her small frame, deciding if she should put a blouse underneath it.

Finally she walks out onto the porch and observes children walking to school, and for a brief moment she wishes that she were a child again being told what to do by both her parents. She watches as a little girl in a plaid dress skips down the street. She wishes she could join her.

Finally, after putting her blue suit on, Precious slides into her BMW, starts her car, and immediately finds the all-news station. There is a special on, and she listens to the commentator talk about DeShan Williams, the rapper, well known as A-Knowledge, who is missing from his Beverly Hills home. He had just signed a seventy-million-dollar deal with a record label. Precious thinks, *They don't seem to be too interested in finding him.*

She remembers that she has candy in her glove compartment and unwraps a piece before sliding out into traffic. She wants to know how her stocks are doing. *Funny,* she thinks, *I did not worry about the stocks one day while I was in a traumatic state of mind.*

Rush-hour traffic seems to be taking much longer than she thought it would. She smiles at a woman in the car next to her when she hears that her stock has gone up by two points.

Then she sees something out of her past. Drinking Scott is walking down the middle of the street. Precious observes him for several minutes. He is walking like he is in the military—shoulders straight, head up, and he looks as though he is marching.

Damn, Precious thinks, *Mom and Dad would always pull him out of the street. I'm not doing it. I'm already late for the meeting this morning.*

A car almost hits him when Precious decides, *Okay, I'll help him, but I don't have all day.* She looks down at her Rolex watch, trying to decide what to do.

"Scott, Scott, what are you doing?"

Drinking Scott continues to march down the street.

Precious gets out of car and screams, "Scott, come here!"

Drinking Scott turns around and starts to march toward Precious. Once he has approached her, he pulls a knife out of his pocket.

Precious is not amused. "Scott, did you take your medication this morning?"

"Call me Major Smith. I was in the Vietnam war, and I am ready to fight the war right here and now."

Precious looks down at her watch again and thinks, *I don't have time to play this game.*

"Scott, get in the car. I'm going to take you home and get some Seraquil in you before you kill yourself. Come on, get in."

Drinking Scott stands there watching Precious for several seconds, realizing that she is in a hurry and knowing that Precious is always serious. He believes that she is way too serious about life.

"Come on, Scott. Let's go."

Drinking Scott gets into the car, and they drive down the street toward his house.

Respectfully, Drinking Scott says, "Sorry about your mom and dad. They saved my life, you know."

"Scott, you can't be walking down the middle of the street swinging a knife at people. I know you, and a lot of people out here know you, but there are a lot of people who don't know you and how kind you are. If the police had seen you swing a knife this morning, they either would have killed you or taken you to jail, and you would have wished that they had killed you. How come you aren't taking your meds?"

"I don't like the way they make me feel."

"Oh, I guess you like the way you look walking down the middle of the street acting like a soldier."

"I am a soldier. You don't understand. I killed innocent people because I was commanded to do it. I even killed children. I drink to forget what I did. But I can't forget it. I flew home after being in the jungle. I was just dropped off on the street and was told to adjust. I can't adjust. Sometimes I had to run for my life. I could hear my heart pounding so hard that I thought I was going to die. I saw my friends killed by land mines, and I can't figure out why my life was spared. The way I see it, ain't nothing wrong with running."

Realizing this conversation is going nowhere, Precious drives silently the next two blocks to his home, alone with her thoughts. *Well, today I feel like running, I would like to run to Mississippi.*

Precious drives up to the place where she thinks Drinking Scott lives. *Is this the home my parents bought for Scott?*

There are car motors on the lawn as well as beer cans and liquor bottles. Two old cars are in the backyard, and the screen door looks as though it might fall off.

Precious starts to ask him for the key, then realizes the door is probably unlocked since no one in his right mind would break into his house.

Inside, the stench permeates the whole house, and Precious is concerned about the smell on her blue suit.

She thinks about what Drinking Scott said in the car and feels sorrowful for his past. His wife has left him—she could not stand being around him anymore.

"Where do you keep your medication?"

"In the bathroom medicine cabinet."

Precious goes into the bathroom and reads the labels on all the meds. She brings them out and demands that Drinking Scott take them. She pours a glass of water for him.

"What happened to your wife?"

"She left me five months ago."

"Where did she go?"

"Cleveland."

Precious thinks, *I don't blame her. I would leave too.*

"Scott, you need to get this place cleaned up. Is Jean still coming over to clean for you?"

"Jean ain't been here in a month."

"Well, you go take a bath and I'm going to prepare breakfast for you. Go!"

Drinking Scott walks into the bathroom and runs water. Precious takes out her cell phone and calls her secretary. Precious changes the time of the meeting, giving her a chance to put services in place for Drinking Scott. While cooking breakfast, she calls Feast on Wheels and asks them to deliver meals to him. She then calls Jean to find out why she isn't coming over to take care of him. Jean tells Precious that Drinking Scott fired her, and she doesn't believe that she is getting enough money to put up with him. Precious promises to pay her an additional hundred dollars a week if she can get over to his house today.

Precious stays until Jean gets there. Drinking Scott is eating breakfast when Jean arrives.

"Okay, you two. Jean, you promise to take care of him?"

"Yep, I'll do it. Where's my money?"

Precious hands her a check. "I'm paying you for last month as well as this month. Take good care of him."

Precious walks over to Drinking Scott, and with a scolding finger she tells him, "Stay out of the street."

Drinking Scott stands up—he appears to be more oriented—and he says, "When are you coming back?"

"I don't know."

"If you don't come back over here to see about me, I'll go over to your condo and march up and down the street."

Precious looks again at her watch. "Okay. Okay. I'll be back real soon. You take your medicine, and I'll see you shortly."

Precious pulls out of the driveway and heads toward the highway that takes her to work every day. As she enters the traffic, which is going rather fast this morning, she glances around at her fellow drivers and wonders about their lives. Just as she is about to get into the fast lane, she observes a car stop and a woman in the passenger side tries to escape. One man in the backseat and another in the front seat seem to be preventing her from leaving. Precious pulls over to the shoulder of the highway and calls her cousin who is a policeman as she tries to take down the license plate number. But the car starts up and soon is out of sight.

"Can I speak with Ryan Jennings?" She is shaking as she is being transferred to his extension.

"Detective Jennings." The voice is strong and businesslike.

"Hello, Ryan. This is your favorite cousin, Precious."

"Hello, sweetheart, how are you doing? The family is gathering at my house tonight. Are you coming over? There was a man who was at my home last night. He asked a lot of questions about you. What, now you have secret admirers?"

"Ryan, listen, I want to report a kidnapping."

"What?"

"I'm on the highway, and I'm on my way into work, and a woman was trying to get out of a car and two men pulled her back in."

"What kind of car was it?"

"It was a deep purple car. I got half of the license plate. Do you want it?"

"Yes. There has been a rash of kidnappings nationally. Give me the number, and I'll follow up on it."

Precious gives him what she has and secretly is disappointed that she isn't able to help out further.

There is a relieved sound in Ryan's voice. "Well, at least now we have some kind of lead. Thank you, baby cousin. Are you coming over tonight?"

"For a minute."

"Maybe that guy will come back. It was something bizarre about that man. Coming up in my house asking about you."

"Jazzy told me about it, Ryan. I don't know who it could have been."

"Are you coming over tonight?"

"I already told you that I would be coming over for a minute. I'm really busy."

"I'm glad you're getting out of the house tonight. If you need help with anything, let me know."

"I will." Precious hangs up the phone a little shaken. She waits several minutes before venturing back into the flow of traffic.

Precious pulls into her parking spot, and she checks to see if her name is still printed on a wall where she has parked for almost four years. *Yep, there it is. Precious Jennings.* Too much has happened in the past two weeks and she wonders seriously if coming in to work was a good idea.

She sits in her car for several minutes as she thinks about how she will respond when her coworkers laugh at her about going to Mississippi. The idea of going to Mississippi is starting to sound better to her. She reflects on what Drinking Scott said to her: *Nothing wrong with running away.* She wonders why two men would strong-arm a helpless woman, and she's sorry she wasn't able to do more for her.

She has a gut feeling that getting out of town for a while will help her recover from the recent deaths and the ongoing tension this town is known for. She would also like to get away from what she believes is her obligation to Drinking Scott, her sister, and the missing Larry.

For a split second, Precious thinks about the Pinnacle Finishing School her mother made her attend. The classes taught her how to walk, sit, and stand, and she uses those graces as she exits the car. She feels she is missing something, and she cannot remember what it is. As she closes the door, the synapses start to connect, and she remembers her burgundy attaché case that she has not looked inside for almost two weeks. She heads to the trunk of her car, brushes the dust off it, places the straps over her shoulder, and heads toward the building.

It does not matter that she is two hours late—Precious simply doesn't care. The receptionist is watching as Precious comes through the door. Precious knows that if anything is going on in the corporation, Kathy knows it first. The expression on Kathy's face will tell her if she is in the line of fire. Precious also knows that Kathy doesn't like her. Precious always smiles at her, and several times she has brought her flowers and candy, yet Precious knows that Kathy has always remained superficial in their interactions. Precious vowed several months ago not to go out of her way for Kathy anymore.

Precious manages to smile as she walks past Kathy's desk.

Kathy pretends to be engrossed in a conversation. She gives Precious an insincere smile, then turns her back to Precious.

At that moment Precious realizes that there is a full-scale war being waged against her today. She passes by twelve people seated in cubicles and smiles and says hello. On their faces is a sense of despair. Most of them she surmises are only working for a paycheck, and if they hit the lottery, all of them would be gone and none of them would give two weeks' notice.

Precious is relieved to walk into her office and closes the door for a moment for a silent prayer. *Lord, please don't let another negative thing happen to me today.*

Morse Smith walks into Precious's office without knocking.

"Welcome back. The agency has fallen apart with you being gone."

"Morse, you worked with Alexandra Davis McBride. What's she like, and what's the city like?"

Morse takes a seat on Precious's desk, and she can see him frowning.

"Well, I didn't get anyplace with her. She's really picky. I told her that I would do anything within my means to help secure the account. I even thought about sleeping with her—I wanted that account." Morse laughs as he thinks about sleeping with the older woman.

"You have got to be kidding." Precious is looking for something on her desk and really isn't paying attention to Morse.

"No, I'm not. That old woman is a difficult client. I knew she wouldn't sleep with all of this." He motions around his stomach as he continues. "She's a Southern lady of means. She can afford to kick people off her account. The kind of money that she's spending with this agency, I bought a house, a new car, and a boat. I would have lost my job and filed for bankruptcy if she had taken her business somewhere else."

"So I need to be on my toes if I go down there?"

"You are going down there. It's already been decided. Yeah, you better be on your toes. That is a sharp old lady."

"Is there anything else I should know?"

"She has a crazy daughter—walks around all day in Dr. Seuss hats and works at the post office. Now her I would pursue, but the girl is just too damn crazy. Alexandra Davis McBride is old, and she's going to leave all that money to that crazy woman. I could show her how to spend it."

Precious wants to get to the heart of the matter, and she wants to do it before the meeting starts. "Is there something strange about the town or the family?"

"Yeah. I couldn't wait for that old woman to fire me. The whole town is strange. The Knights of Darkness run the city, and the Black people down there are scared to death of them. Alexandra Davis McBride is the organizer of the Black farmers, and they want to get fair prices for their products. They want to sell their products for the same price as White farmers do. Most of the Black farmers are going bankrupt. It's just a matter of time before something's going to happen, and I'm just glad that I'm not going to be there."

Morse walks toward the door and turns around with a somber expression. "If I were you, I would turn this assignment down. It's going to be a blood bath in that town, and I wouldn't want to be there when that happens."

Morse walks out of the room, leaving Precious there to momentarily think about the project.

Trina walks into Precious's office. "Oh, you are here. What time will the meeting start?"

Precious scans her desk for files before she says, "I think I can manage a meeting in ten minutes."

Every single time Precious is out of the office for any length of time, there are meetings about her, and those meetings are normally to Precious's annihilation. Precious knows that she's one of the hardest working managers in the office, but she knows that if the staff could figure out a way to harness her talents without bringing five people in to replace her, they would.

She already knows what the meeting is about—the Alexandra Davis McBride account—and she takes the information she has on this lady out of her file. She scrutinizes the information and considers what Morse has just told her about the town.

Precious takes out her compact and brushes her face before venturing down the hall to what she considers her doom.

Everyone is already seated when Precious walks into the room.

"Sorry I had to change the meeting. I had a family emergency." Precious walks audaciously to a seat at the far end of the room, away from the president of the firm, Dwight DeVeux, who is chairing the meeting. She opens her folder, deciding not to look up.

"Precious," DeVeux says, directing his attention to her, "we at

DeVeux Advertising are sorry about the death of your parents. Although we sent a plant to the funerals, we also wanted to give you one. We would like to give you this *alocasia colocasia* plant." He places a large elephant ear plant on the table and motions for her to come pick it up. After Precious thanks everyone in the room, she returns to her seat and sets the plant on the floor. She thinks, *Damn plant, now there's something else I have to be responsible for.*

DeVeux continues to talk to the ten people gathered around the table. "As you know, Morse is no longer on the McBride account, and I need a volunteer sales representative to service the account. Of course anyone who volunteers will be compensated for all of your out-of-pocket expenses."

The room is quiet as all eyes are on Precious, then those same eyes dart back to Mr. DeVeux.

Precious thinks, *I'm not sure there was a meeting that elected me to service this account, so I'm not going to volunteer to do it.*

Mona speaks up and says, "Well, I talked to Precious about taking this account. It would give her a chance to get out of town for a while."

Precious speaks before thinking and says, "There are so many other people who know this account much better than I do. I've just gotten back, and I'm not abreast of the intricacies of this client. Also, I have clients that I haven't seen in a month, and their ads bring in millions of dollars, so I would respectfully ask that someone else handle this account."

DeVeux sits up straight and directs his response to Precious. "Precious, I don't mind telling you that you are the best sales representative in this agency, and you might be the best sales representative in the state. If you take this account, I'll give you a week's vacation and send you to that spa that you women like to go to." He smiles proudly at her.

Precious thinks, *Here he goes, trying to punk me again with a one-week vacation and spa privileges to a place where he's handling their advertising. My trip to the South won't cost him a thing.*

Precious clears her throat. "Could I speak to you alone, in your office?"

"Why sure you can." He turns to the others in the room and announces, "This meeting is over."

After all the financial haggling, Precious has a deal that she can be happy with. The other staff members will handle her clients and Precious will continue to receive half the commissions for those accounts. She will receive the full commission from the McBride account as well.

"Will that make you happy, Precious?" Mr. DeVeux says.

"No. I want to be a full partner."

"I can't do that."

"Well then, I'm not going. Maybe I'll start my own business, let people in the state know that I'm branching out on my own."

"Okay, damn it, but you better stop blackmailing me."

Precious is happy, but she doesn't show it. "Put all of this in a letter, and I'll stop by your assistant's office before I leave for Mississippi in two days. It was nice doing business with you." Precious extends her hand, and Dwight DeVeux stands there just gazing at her, as though a challenger in a heavyweight championship fight has just beaten him up.

Precious goes to the door and turns around. "Just one more thing I want you to do."

"What is that? Give you my salary?"

"Don't be silly. I want you to call a meeting and tell the staff that I'm going to be a partner in your business, today."

Dwight DeVeux shakes his head. "I'll do it if you'll have dinner with me tonight."

"Hell, no, I won't have dinner with you, and make the damn

announcement today." She leaves the room and slams the door.

Somewhere in Mississippi

The General is taking a walk through the woods when the Sergeant approaches him.

"Sir, we got all the people you requested on the list."

The General keeps walking. "We're going to bring them all here. No one will ever find them here."

"Are you talking about constructing a building?"

The General walks around several trees, then states, "What I'm talking about is an underground jail. I want you to bring men out here and dig a big enough hole where five or six people can walk around comfortably. I want you to put in a glass ceiling, a retractable glass, you know, like the sunroofs on cars? Then on top of the glass I want you to put a canvas that will either roll up or down with a touch of a button. You will understand the plan later."

"Sir, we're having problems with the rapper DeShan."

"What's the problem?"

"He stopped eating yesterday. He said he wouldn't eat any more until he is free."

The General knocks down a small tree in anger. "What do they like to eat?"

"What do you mean by what do they like to eat?"

"You know, the um … them?"

The Sergeant hunches his shoulders as he thinks about it. "I suppose they like chicken wings and forty ounces."

"Get him that then."

The Sergeant walks out of the forest and back to his car.

Two hours later the Sergeant is back. "He still won't eat, General. He said he would rather starve to death than have you make a mockery out of his art form."

The General is surprised. "Did he tell you that?"

"Well, no. He used other words."

"What words did he use?"

The Sergeant is uncomfortable as he says, "He told me I could take this forty-ounce and chicken wings and stick it ..."

"I know what he said. I want you to see this picture."

The Sergeant gazes at the picture.

The General says, "DeShan has a sensitivity to women like this. I want you to follow her for a while. She's pretty smart. We're going to kidnap her too."

The Sergeant looks at the picture, then at the address, and finally says, "This should be easy enough."

Chapter 3

Precious goes back into her office and shoves the plant to a corner of the room, then throws the file back into the cabinet. She knows that DeVeux is serious about going out with her, even though he has a wife and two children at home. In her heart she wishes she had someone to talk to about starting her own business. Jazzy doesn't understand why Precious would want to give up a job making six figures a year just to start a business that might fail.

If Precious mentions one word of branching out to anyone in this town, the news would get back to DeVeux before she could decide her company's logo.

There on her desk is a candy bar. She chews slowly, enjoying the chocolate and nuts. She collapses into her chair and puts her head on her desk. She feels a little lethargic and irritated as she thinks about always catering to other people's feelings. It was her parents who decided that she should go to college; it was her parents who thought that she should come home and work in a business locally.

It was her father who talked to Dwight DeVeux about hiring her. Now that they are gone, she is faced with what she really wants to do, and she has no idea what that is. She feels as though she is in a huge valley with forty different paths to take, and there is no one around to advise her as to what direction to go. For the first time in her life, she feels so alone in the decisions she will have to make.

Suddenly she has another daydream. Her mother is sitting comfortably on the couch across the room.

"So you blame your father and me for everything, huh?"

"Well, yeah. I never wanted to see this city again once I graduated from college."

"We didn't twist your arm to make you come back. You came back on your own."

"Yeah, I know. I have to blame it on someone."

Her mother hands her a mirror and tells her to blame the person in the mirror.

"Congratulations on your promotion."

"I would rather be in the south of France."

"Sweetheart, you are where you're supposed to be, going to places that you're supposed to go."

"I don't want to go to Mississippi."

"Why?"

"Because it's just another place where people want to send me."

"Precious, you're in the middle of something that's going to have a lifetime effect on you. Other than your family, have you ever been in the middle of something that changed your life?"

"No."

"If you stay here in this city, in this job, you're going to remain the same and, in addition, you're going to have a nervous breakdown, and it won't be a pretty sight. Remember, I know you."

"Yeah, but if I go to Mississippi, something terrible is going to happen. I just feel it."

"Does your instinct tell you not to go?"

"No."

"Then go there. Go to Mississippi. You won't hear from me any-more. Remember what I told you before. Listen to what people are say-ing to you, and good-bye, my love."

Precious drifts off to sleep, and when she wakes up, she checks her watch. It is now ten minutes later. She searches the room for her mother. There is no one there but her. She thinks again about going to Mississippi and all the preparation going into the move. Precious has to pay bills, go to the dry cleaners, and ask neighbors to pick up her mail. She stares out over the city and the beach a block from her office.

Precious has another illusion as she hears, "Please help me."

"Who are you?"

"I'm the person you saw in the car, and I need your help. Please help me."

"Where are you now?"

"Please help me." The voice sounds distraught, and Precious gazes around the room, searching for the troubled voice.

It has taken Precious a lifetime to get to this moment in her life, and she wonders if she is off her rocker and if she would be better off to stay in Michigan or go to Mississippi right now. She cannot remember when or how her personality deteriorated or for what reason. She can't stand the thought of having visions and thinks about talking to a psychiatrist before leaving town.

Precious has managed to alienate almost everyone on staff at the advertising agency. Although she has been with the agency for four years, she still feels as though she's an outsider, and being a partner will make her feel even more estranged from the staff. She wonders if this is contributing to her seeing visions.

Precious has never once taken her eye off her goal. She scans her office, which is big enough for her couch and two tables. It also has a view for which others would die. When she first moved into the office, she believed it was heaven. Now she believes that it has become her hell, and she wonders if there is more to life than just pushing papers around.

The phone rings, and when she picks it up, she is surprised. It is Larry, the man she honestly loves. She takes off her clip earrings so that she can hear him clearly.

"Hi, Precious. I was at both your parents' funerals. My secretary sent flowers to the church. I just wanted to tell you how sorry I am about their deaths. I was wondering if I could take you to a concert tomorrow night. Joe Sample and Layla Hathaway and Norman Brown are going to be there at the theater."

Precious thinks, *You are always staying on the periphery of my life. How come you didn't comfort me during the funerals at the most trau - matic moments in my life?*

Although Precious has all these questions, she's just glad that he has called. She loves jazz and searches her calendar. She continues to talk as she searches the computer for her appointments. He is the only man who can cause her to feel anxious. She taps her pen on the desk, irritated that the computer is taking too long. She says while waiting for her appointments to come up, "Thank you. I was going to send you a thank-you letter. How come you didn't let me know that you were there?"

"I'm no good around things like that. I got out of there as soon as I could."

"Well, thanks for the flowers."

"Oh, I don't care about that. It wasn't enough. Would you like to go to the concert with me?"

Precious doesn't say anything. She has a meeting tomorrow night with a client. She considers canceling the appointment.

"I just moved into my first home." Larry is proud that he has bought his first home. "We could go over to my house after the concert. I could whip up a nice after-party snack for just you and me. How about it?" he says seductively. Every time she hears him talk like this, she is ready to give in to him with everything she has. The problem is that once she does give in to him, she doesn't see him for another month.

"I don't know about a concert right now. I've got to leave in a couple of days. I've got to go to Mississippi, and at this point I don't know when I'm coming back."

"Well, I'd like to take you out to make your last days in the city well worth coming back for. I have a box seat in the amphitheater. I'm going to have food catered in. I really want to show you a good time before you leave. Man, you've hung in there with your family. Let them go tomorrow night and have some fun. Just imagine, we can eat, make love, and watch one of the coolest brothers and one sister in jazz without being bothered by anyone. Please say yes."

"Please, Larry, although that sounds really good, I ain't making love to you. Please." She thinks, *I don't know why I'm lying. I know as soon as he kisses me in my ear, I'm gone.*

"Okay, forget about making love, but we could have a good time listening to some good music." Larry thinks, *I'm going to have to give you some extra tender loving care to get you in the mood.*

Precious says, "Okay, I'll go. I need a change. Do you want me to meet you there?"

"No, baby, chivalry ain't dead. I'm coming to pick you up. You remember that short red backless dress you wore to your party your mother came to and those stiletto red heels? Could you please do a brother a favor and wear them again? Man, you were really slammin' that night. Could you wear your hair down? I like the way it bounces when you walk with your back shaking all over everything."

Precious thinks, *What the hell have I gotten myself into?*

But she says, "I'll see what I can do."

Precious goes to the gym and works out for an hour. She runs on the treadmill as though she is running from her life. She remembers what Drinking Scott said and wonders, if the time would come, if she could run for her life. Sweat pours down her face as her muscles start to ache, and she tries to regulate her breathing. There are people running on both sides of her. The music is blaring Earth, Wind and Fire's "September," and several people who are not working out take time to dance to the music.

There is a woman running next to Precious with a short Afro who appears to be more underweight than Precious, who has never been able to compete with her. This woman seems to delight in running faster than anyone in the gym. After thirty minutes, Precious is ready to hit the showers. She marvels at the woman's tenacity because when Precious comes out of the shower and is ready to leave, this woman is still running. Precious surmises that when she has eaten dinner and has washed up all the dishes, this woman will still probably be at the gym running. She makes up her mind that she is going to ask this lady what makes her run for such a long time. Precious has been intrigued with her. She wants to be able to run like that someday. Precious concludes that this lady has a purpose in her running.

After showering, Precious walks over to the Manna Health Food Store, which is located in the same complex as the gym. She buys organic vegetables and fruits. The manager of the store pulls her to the side to discuss the cranberries and how he has heard that they may reduce strokes. He goes on to talk for at least ten minutes about how researchers will be developing cranberries into stroke-fighting drugs and a nutraceutical. Precious believes that he covertly thinks she is special, and when she is talking to him, she feels as though she is the most important person in the world. She has not seen him get excited about cranberries or any other produce with anyone else the way he does with her, and she has been coming into the Manna Health Food Store for over ten years. The store manager's enthusiasm about the produce encourages Precious, and she is glad that she is a vegetarian.

Precious notices a man is following her, and she stops on her way out of the store and then comes back in. She pretends that she is examining a cranberry as she watches the man who seems to be gazing at her. She debates if she should tell the store manager. This man is exactly like the person that Jazzy and Ryan described to her. Precious takes out her cell phone and walks out of the store and runs into the woman who runs faster than anyone else at the gym. Precious closes the cell phone and her concentration shifts. When she looks up again, the man has disappeared.

Precious smiles and says, "I marvel at the way that you run. Are you a model?"

The strange and beautiful woman laughs and says, "No. I am from Liberia. There has been civil unrest in my country, and I've had to learn how to run to save my life and my family's lives."

Precious is stunned. "How long have you been here?"

"A year."

"Do you know anyone here?"

"No. It is a lonely place."

Precious, who is dead tired, feels sorry for the woman and says, "Would you like to go to the coffee shop? I'm buying." Precious s e a r c hes around the mall to see if the man is still following her, and she doesn't see him.

"Yes, I would love to."

After ordering, they take a seat close to the mall's hallway so that they can watch the passing people.

"My name is Binta. It means 'with God.'"

Precious says, "My name is Precious. It means, according to my mother, that I am special."

Binta smiles and says, "Yes, you do seem special. I have been watching you run. You run like a Westerner."

Precious starts smiling. "What do you mean?"

"You run pretty."

Precious somehow doesn't feel as though this is a compliment.

"In my country, it is both hot and dangerous. I don't run pretty, I run for my life. I wish that I could run pretty too. You look as though you have never had danger in your life. I am happy for you."

Precious tries to remember one time that she has had danger in her life and has a hard time remembering something. She wants to tell Binta the time that she was almost raped in the parking lot of her condo and how she got out of the situation, but somehow this episode does not compare to what Binta has gone through.

Precious's third eye tells her that this woman has seen some things in her life that Precious would not have survived.

"My family was killed in the war. I was raped by sixteen soldiers and left for dead. I didn't die—I refused to die. I know you think that you couldn't do what I did, but you have a look, and even though I don't know you, I know your kind. I run because I know that I have to stay strong. I run because I need to stay healthy. You never know what might happen to you. It is always wise to be energetic and prepared."

While driving home, Precious thinks about what Binta has said to her. She knows that she will never forget that conversation. She thinks, *I run pretty because I don't have the same hardships. My parents died, but they died a natural death.* The coroner had told Precious after the funeral that her mother died of a heart attack. Precious knows that her mother died of a broken heart.

Precious goes to Ryan's house on her way home. The music is blaring and people are all over the house. There are all kinds of food on the table.

Precious asks Ryan, "Did you find that woman?"

"No, I didn't, but there's a woman missing. Her name is Jessica Zellman, and she's an activist."

Precious listens intently. She tries to decide if she should tell Ryan about a vision she had in her office about this woman. Precious thinks twice before deciding not to tell Ryan about the illusion. Instead she says, "I don't know the name. What is she known for?"

"Well, Michigan has become a dumping site, and other states and countries bring their trash here. She has been protesting and has quite a following. I think you saw something today. We tracked down the license number you gave us. The car was stolen."

Precious almost drops her glass of wine.

"Well, if you hear anything, please call me on my cell phone. I'm going to be in Mississippi for a while. I want to know how this one turns out."

"Why are you going to Mississippi?"

"I need a break and to have a woman renew a contract."

"Well, you be careful going down there. What part of Mississippi are you going to?"

"Star, Mississippi."

Ryan stops what he is doing and says, "Don't they have the Knights of Darkness?"

"Yep. I've heard that."

Ryan takes Precious's hand as he continues to talk. "They're danger-ous, so stay away from them. Do what you have to do and come back home. I mean it, it is serious." Ryan shakes his head, disapproving of her traveling to an unsafe town and being so far away from her family.

After driving home, Precious takes out her red dress and wraps it around her. She swirls around the room, excited about going out with Larry. Even though she hasn't had any sleep, she is too excited to go to bed. She stays up most of the night organizing the clothes she plans to take to Mississippi with her. Several times, her thoughts drift back to the woman she believes was being kidnapped in the car, and she is saddened that she was not able to help her.

Chapter 4

April 3

The next morning, Precious calls in sick. She can barely get the words out of her mouth. She places the phone back on the receiver and turns over in bed.

She has only slept two hours when the phone rings again. It's Jazzy. They talk for several minutes. Precious tells her that she is going out tonight, and Jazzy tells Precious that she is having a good time in the Bahamas.

The phone rings again just when Precious is about to fall asleep again.

"Hey, Precious. Hello. This is Terrance. Remember, you told me that you thought I need to be on medication?"

Precious sits up in bed. "Have you been following me?"

"Well, I went over to your cousin's house. I thought I would see you there."

Precious checks the time. "You know it's against the law to be stalking people."

"Precious, I'm not stalking you. I just want to know where you're going. You know, since you told me I needed medication, I went to a psychiatrist, and he put me on lithium, and I feel really happy now."

Precious gets up and walks over to the window and looks out. "Are you somewhere near my house now?"

"Why, yes. I thought I might take you out to lunch."

"Look, Terrance, leave me alone. I have a boyfriend. Don't make me call the police on you."

"So does that mean you won't have lunch with me?"

"Let me tell you something, Terrance. If I walk out of my house and see you anywhere, I'm calling the police. If you call me one more time, I'm going to have my cousin Ryan meet you at your house. Are we clear on that?"

"Yeah. I guess you don't want to see me again."

Precious, realizing that she won't be able to sleep anymore, says, "Well, you are clear, and if you call me again, I'm real clear that I'll call the police."

Precious hangs up the phone and starts packing for her trip, more than ready to leave town for a while.

When Larry rings Precious's doorbell, she thinks, *I've only had two hours of sleep today.* Larry is handsome, a well-educated man, but a little uptight about life. No one is sure what nationality he belongs to—he has always been able to blend into any setting. He is six-four and weighs about 185 pounds. Most people who are introduced to him wonder openly about his ethnic background. He never answers and has told Precious that he doesn't want to be pinned down. When he is talking on the phone, his Ivy League voice doesn't give him away. Precious wonders if he really knows who he is.

When she answers the door, Larry can't take his eyes off her. He is dressed elegantly, in a three-piece blue suit and a red tie with a red hanky dangling from the pocket. He looks as though he is made of gold—his confidence adds to his look of prosperity. He has a condescending aura, which makes people around him ill at ease. He is holding both chocolate candy and flowers. After Precious accepts the presents, she opens up the candy and chooses a piece before giving

Larry a hug. He looks as though he is in a hurry, even though the show doesn't start for two hours and Precious lives only two miles from the theater.

"Would you like a glass a wine?" Precious says, hoping this might loosen him up some.

"No. You know I don't drink."

Precious takes out a crystal goblet and pours herself a drink. "Well, I need a drink."

When Precious and Larry walk into the arena, all eyes are on them. An usher escorts them to their box seats. When they walk into the room, there are all kinds of vegetables, fruit, and fresh fish.

Larry hands the usher money, then asks, "Could you please leave us alone? We will not need anything else."

The man acts as though he hasn't heard Larry as he says, "I just want to show you several things." He opens up the refrigerator and says, "You may help yourself." He then shows them how to open and close the drapes and how to control the sound, then smiles and leaves the room. Even though Larry is a season-ticket holder, this same man shows him where everything is every time that Larry shows up, and Larry doesn't stop him.

Norman Brown comes on stage and starts playing a classic song by Janet Jackson, "That's the Way Love Goes." Excitement fills the air, and Precious starts to dance seductively to the music. Her head is back, her arms swaying like a ballerina, her hair dangling, and her body is moving freely. *At last, I feel the freedom,* she thinks as she continues to move around the room. *Maybe Mississippi won't be so bad.*

Larry sits on the couch, watching her body move. His temperature is rising as he scrutinizes her moves. Larry asks Precious for a dance, and they dance around the room. He kisses her passionately. She can feel his manliness rising, and she pushes him back.

When Norman Brown plays "Reasons" on his sexy-sounding saxophone, Larry leads Precious to the couch, and she follows willingly. He turns down the lights in the room. Precious believes that maybe she might be giving Larry his way as he starts to kiss her again in places he hasn't been in a while. She remembers his every move, and she knows them by heart. She even knows when and where he's going to make his final move. She also remembers that once he makes his classic moves that she will not see him again for another month or two. She abruptly gets up off the couch and walks over to the window to listen to Joe Sample and Layla Hathaway.

"What's wrong with you?" Larry says, almost angry.

"I'm not into casual sex anymore."

"Baby, I'm not into casual sex either. I want to get closer to you."

"I don't feel the same. Baby, you haven't done anything for me. You just showed up out of the blue."

"How about this?" Larry motions around the room. "I don't do this for just anybody, you know."

"I know. Why are you doing it for me? I haven't seen you in months. Why now?"

"Well, I just may want to marry you."

Precious thinks, *I've heard this before.* "Sweetheart, your telling me that you may want to marry me ain't working anymore. When I'm in Mississippi, I want you to act like you wanna be with me."

"What do you mean?"

"I want you to call me, do things couples do when they're in love and are apart. If you still wanna get married, treat me like a queen. Don't spend a zillion dollars on a concert and then don't show up for months. I deserve better. Learn how to be consistent."

Larry knows where this conversation is going and tries one last time to change her mind. His kisses her softly in her ear, and Precious pulls away. *Damn,* he thinks, *this has always worked before.* "So I'm not going to be nestling in your nest tonight, huh?"

"No, you're not. Please don't make me repeat myself. I deserve much more than this concert. Let me tell you what's going to happen if I let it. You're going to give it all you've got, which is really good. But then I won't hear from you for another one or two months, and at that time you'll talk about getting married again. Be consistent."

Larry thinks, *This is consistent.* He looks resigned to not having sex tonight. He then thinks, *It's about time you wised up. I need a challenge, and you surely haven't provided one nor confronted me in this relationship. I have a little more respect for you now, but it's going to be hard having you so far away.*

"I wore this slinky little dress for you. Come on. Give me more, and I'll give you more."

"What more do you want?"

"I want your mind to be with me when you're not physically with me. I want you to man up and take this relationship to the next level."

"Well, let's talk." He leans in closer to Precious. "When you go to Mississippi, you're going to be sick of me. I'm going to call you every day. I want you to know that I love you, and this night I pledge to respect you, and you will be my woman forever."

Precious smiles and says, "Now we'll see, won't we? Right now I prefer to watch the concert tonight."

Larry smiles. "I'll take you to the airport tomorrow."

Somewhere in Mississippi

The Sergeant is amazed at the size of the structure and how much work has already been done. "I can't believe the progress you've made."

The General says, "I'm serious about this. We still have some more work to do. I'm not sure how I'm going to handle the plumbing. I guess I'll ask Hal and his boys to do it. Where is he?"

"He's in Pleasant Ville right now."

"Sergeant, get him back here and have him get this work done. I want it done before the woman is snatched. By the way, what do you know about her?"

The Sergeant smiles. "She will be taking a trip soon."

The General moves timber out of the way as he says, "For now, keep an eye on her."

Chapter 5

April 4

Precious sits in first class of Fusion Airlines, gazing out of the window. The night before, after Larry dropped Precious off, instead of going to sleep, she went to the All Night Nail Salon for a manicure. She gazes down at her nails and thinks how beautiful they are. She had the manicurist redo her nails several times before she got to the right color, and now she is pleased with how her nails look.

She tries to remember if she has forgotten anything. Precious has set up an account for Drinking Scott's care, and she has a neighbor watering her plants and picking up the mail that isn't forwarded to her in Mississippi.

Larry has told her that he will call her every day. If he does, Precious will marry him when she returns from her business trip. She isn't sure how long it will take her to convince this woman to sign the contract.

She believes that she has everything she needs for the account, including the charisma and the reduced rates specially designed for this account. She thinks, *How can I lose?*

The plane will land in Atlanta, Georgia, in less than two hours. Precious has decided to rent a BMW in Atlanta and then drive to Mississippi from there. Atlanta is the only city close to Star, Mississippi, which has the kind of BMW Precious wants to drive. She checks her Cartier watch. It's ten in the morning. She then calculates her time in Atlanta and believes that after eating lunch and picking up her rental car, she should be on the outskirts of Star, Mississippi, where she will be renting a cottage near a body of water, by 5:30.

Precious sits back in her first-class comfortable seat and looks out over the clouds in the sky. She wonders momentarily if her mother is her guardian angel as she looks out over the clouds for her spirit. She believes that somehow her mother is accompanying her to this part of the country where her mother and grandmother grew up. She opens the box of candy that Larry gave her, and she enjoys several pieces while in deep contemplation.

"Ladies and gentlemen, I am Captain Brooks, and we will soon be landing in Atlanta, where the temperature is 85 degrees on this beautiful spring day. There are beautiful stratus clouds. We will be descending in a few minutes, and you will be on the ground in twenty minutes. We are ahead of schedule. Enjoy your stay in this fine city."

Precious takes out her compact and looks at herself in the mirror, then brushes her hair back one last time and reapplies her Perfect Plum lipstick.

Precious is greeted at the airport entrance by the BMW leasing agent. He is an elegant-looking middle-age man wearing a Stacy Adams suit, carrying a folder of paperwork in his large hands. He is impeccably dressed with a goatee that enhances his appearance.

"Hello. My name is Philip Wright, and your burgundy 760 BMW is waiting for you out front. All you need to do is sign these papers."

Precious studies the contract carefully for several minutes, then asks, "Do I have a sunroof?"

"Yes."

"What kind of sound system do I have?"

"You have the very best of everything. Come on. Let me show you.

This car would cost you around $125,000 if you decided to buy one."

Precious smiles and says, "I have a car just like this one at home."

Philip is impressed with the beautiful Precious and takes her by her arm and escorts her to the car.

"Where are you going?" he asks. The question seems more personal than professional.

"I'm going to a little town called Star in Mississippi."

"You're what?"

"I'm going to Star."

Philip sounds concerned as he says, "That town is having a lot of problems with church bombings, and there is a problem with the Knights of Darkness. Are you going to be there by yourself?"

"Yes, but I can take care of myself."

Philip's forehead wrinkles as he says, "I bet you've never met any-one like these people before. Please be careful about how you interact with people there. They're not used to strong women like you appear to be. I've got your address at the cottage. I'll be checking up on you.

"The newspaper has been filled with crimes against People of Color there. There have been several suspicious hangings in the past three years. The Black farmers over there are going to Washington to request the government's help because not many of the farmers will have any money left—most of them will be bankrupt by the end of this crop year. What are you going over there for?"

"I'm a partner in an advertising agency, and I'm going over there to talk to a client about signing a new contract."

"How long are you going to be there?"

"As soon as the contract is signed, I'm out of there."

"Precious, I don't know you, but please be careful in regard to what you say, to whom you say it, and where you say it. People don't like to look bad. You're a beautiful, sophisticated, well-educated woman who is driving a BMW. You're everything they want to stop. You're talking to people they loathe. Please take care of your business and get out of town as soon as you can."

"I'm not leaving until she signs the contract."

"Make her sign and then leave. I'll be checking on you."

"You mean you'll be checking up on your car."

"What I mean is that you don't know what you're about to get yourself involved with. I'll be checking up on you."

After Philip spends half an hour with Precious, showing her the updated features of the car and what the contract really means, Precious signs the papers. When she goes to get into the car, Philip reappears with a tray of fresh fruit.

"I thought you might like this on your way to Mississippi." Precious smiles and says "thanks," and he places the tray of freshly cut fruit on the seat next to her. She looks down at it and finds pomegranate, pineapple, guava, mango, papaya, and lychee.

The navigational driving system points her in the direction of Mississippi. Precious finds the sounds of jazz maestro Alfonzo Blackwell playing and turns the sound up in the car. Precious can barely keep her eyes open. Even though there is beautiful scenery, she finds herself nodding off several times, and she can hardly wait to get to her cottage so that she can sleep. She starts to think about the kidnapping she witnessed and becomes upset once again.

Precious looks into her rearview mirror and sees the same car that has been behind her for the last hundred miles. She tries to peer inside the car from her rearview window, but is unable to make out the person in the automobile. She continues to glance into the mirror when her car veers off the highway and she almost runs into a tree. She is ten miles from the city limit of Tuscaloosa, Alabama. The car behind her speeds past her without stopping, and Precious takes a good look inside the car and sees an elderly woman. Precious laughs to herself and thinks that she is too paranoid. She wonders why she is so mistrustful at the moment.

She stops and gets out of the car. *No damage,* she thinks. She checks the heel of her shoe, which is still intact. The shoes cost Precious two thousand dollars. When she saw them in Italy last year she couldn't rest until the shoes were on her feet. She looks down at them and thinks, *They were well worth the trouble of buying them.* She then checks her fingernails and thinks, *All is well.*

She sits for several minutes before starting the car. She looks toward the highway to see if she can locate the other car, and it appears to be gone from view.

An unfamiliar light comes on inside the car. She decides to get it checked out in the next town. She checks her map and realizes she should be driving into Tuscaloosa in several minutes. She maneuvers her way around the city, searching for a service station, then mysteriously the light goes off. Precious drives into a service station and, after several minutes, the mechanic tells her that he can't find anything wrong.

Precious pays him, and once again she is on the road. She thinks she can get into her cottage by 8:30. It is now 3:30, and she stills has several hundred miles to go. Finally, around seven o'clock, Precious pulls onto a country road that leads to both the cottage and Alexandra Davis McBride's home. She goes several miles down a red clay dirt road until her car stops. Precious tries to start it several times, but nothing happens. She removes her cell phone from her purse and tries to make a call, and the phone goes dead. She spies a farmhouse about two miles away and decides to walk.

Precious locks her car before leaving. The red clay is in her hair. Precious steps into a large blob of cow manure and breaks the heel of her shoe in the process. *Damn,* she thinks. Precious begins to talk out loud angrily to the cornfields as she passes. "I haven't had any sleep in two weeks, my car has stopped in the middle of nowhere, I can't remember the last time I had sex, my heel has come off my two-thousand-dollar shoes, I work for a jackass, and it is hot as hell down here." Dirt collects on her face, and the hours and money that she spent in the beauty salon have been for nothing.

There are cornfields all around her as she spies a larger-than-life tractor coming toward her. She stops as the tractor comes to a halt beside her.

A very tall, dark-skinned, handsome man dismounts and walks toward her. She notices the large cowboy boots, cowboy hat, and his blue-checkered shirt. He looks as though he is dressed up for a country square dance, and Precious has just been spotted as the suitable boogie partner.

He notices the beautiful shape and the attractive face behind the dirt that has collected on her nose and hair.

"Hello, Miss." He tilts his hat and asks, "Are you having some trouble here?"

"Yeah. My car just stopped. I've got to get to a phone."

"I'll take you down the road, and you can use the phone there."

Precious looks curiously at the handsome stranger, trying to decide whether she can trust him or not.

"I don't know … maybe I'll just walk down the road a bit. My cell phone should work then."

"Madam, if you can't get your cell phone to work, I don't mind taking you to a phone. I ain't gonna hurt you. My name is Michael, and I grew up around here. Everybody in this town knows me. Here, let me show you my Boy Scout medals. I carry them around just for cases like this one."

Precious studies his face several seconds before replying, "You know, you're pretty funny. Do you work on the side as a stand-up comic?"

"Yep. Every Saturday night. That's how I make my money. You know a brother gotta get paid."

Precious remembers the danger and studies the handsome stranger's face one last time before she says, "Okay, I'll let you take me to a phone."

"Oh, I'm thrilled that you're going to give me this privilege," he says sarcastically. "Get in."

He opens the door for her, and she climbs inside the cabin and breaks a nail on her way in. She is about to scream as she looks down at the broken nail. She searches her purse, trying to find a file, and remembers that she packed it away in her luggage. Precious notices that the stranger is watching her and hides the finger and tries to appear in control of her emotions.

She feels comfortable as he plays the old Motown sounds over the sounds of the slow-moving tractor. The air-conditioning in the tractor feels good as she leans back and listens to the music.

"So what are you doing out this way?"

"I'm here to meet with Mrs. Alexandra Davis McBride. Do you know her?"

"Yes, I know her."

"Do you know her well?"

"What do you mean by that? Do you ever know someone well?"

"Yep. I know several people well."

"No you don't," Michael says, sneaking several peeks at Precious. "All you can ever do in life is to know yourself well."

Precious turns to him and asks, "What are you, some sort of philosopher or something?"

He turns to her over the sounds of the Temptations who are singing "Ain't Too Proud to Beg" and says, "Yep, I've been called that."

The tractor continues to move unhurriedly down the old dirt road.

"Where are you from?"

Precious moves around uneasily in the tractor, trying to find a comfortable spot. The bumps in the dirt road are starting to take their toll on her behind. She thinks, *This tractor is moving too slow,* and says proudly, "I'm from Shalom, Michigan."

"What do you do there?"

"I'm a partner in an advertising firm."

"How much do you make a year?"

"None of your business."

"Is it over a hundred thousand dollars a year?"

Precious does not say anything.

"Well, it must be some money 'cause you've got to have some money to drive what you're driving." He turns to look at Precious. "That damn car ain't even practical. You can't plow a field with it, and I bet it cost over a hundred thousand dollars, and look at it stuck on a back country road. It ain't good for nothin'."

Precious takes a deep breath, and the anger continues to mount, even though she has tried to stop talking.

"I'm not going to plow the back forty with my BMW. As a matter of fact, I'm not going to be plowing around a field at three miles an hour for eight hours a day for twenty-five cents a day. That isn't practical, and it surely won't make me any money."

"Well, if I wasn't plowing the back forty for stuck-up people like you, you wouldn't have any food to eat so that you could go to a job where people don't respect you, so that you can make more money to spend on useless pieces of junk that don't work to impress one-dimensional folk.

"Let me out!"

"Where are you going? You don't know anyone, and all those credits cards and money in your purse won't get you what you need right now. But me, a simple farm boy, and a thirty-five-thousand-dollar tractor will get you from point A to point B at three miles an hour."

Precious tries to remain silent as Michael continues to drive the tractor slowly down the dirt road. There are no cars coming or going in either direction.

Somewhere in Mississippi

The General is out working on the structure, along with sixty other men. The Sergeant smiles as they greet each other.

The Sergeant says, "Well, things are moving as scheduled. Is DeShan eating?"

"Yep. He started eating today. He's going to be a handful. I think we're going to be able to deal with the rest of them, but he's a problem. What's going on with the woman?"

The Sergeant smiles again. "I figure if we're going to make our move, we should do it after the meeting."

The General shakes the Sergeant's hand. "You've done a fine job. Yes, after the meeting we'll seize her."

Chapter 6

It seems as though hours have passed instead of minutes as Precious rides slowly toward the little farmhouse. Precious is shocked as Michael drives leisurely down the road past the farmhouse.

"Where are you going? You're passing the farmhouse."

The Temptations continue to sing "Please Return Your Love to Me" as the tractor continues to slowly move down the secluded road.

Michael is quiet and Precious shouts, "Right there. I want to go right there."

"No, I'll take you to Mrs. McBride's house. It's only a mile farther down the road. The people who live there are not friendly, and they might not let you use their phone."

Precious does not want to meet Mrs. McBride until she is cleaned up. Precious does not want any snares in her plan, which is to be out of this scary little town in a few days.

"Could you just drop me off at my cottage and I'll have the car towed to a service center?"

"No. I have a better plan. I'll drop you off at the mansion, and I'll take a friend who is a mechanic back to the car."

Precious hates that this man who she doesn't know has so much power and control over her life.

"I would like to freshen up before I meet Mrs. McBride."

"What for? She's not home. She went to Jackson. She'll be home tomorrow."

"You could have told me that in the first place."

"This is the first place."

"What am I supposed to be doing while you're off fixing my car? Wait ... I don't know you. Why should I give my keys to you?"

"Ask the people at Mrs. McBride's house. They'll tell you that I'm an honorable person who would never take advantage of a damsel in distress."

For some reason, Precious believes him and says nothing more for the rest of the ride.

Precious presses her head against the glass and wishes that she were anywhere but in the tractor with Michael. She thinks, *I don't know how I'm going to ride one more mile in this tractor with this man.*

Just then Michael starts singing to the Temptations' "Just My Imagination." This irritates Precious, and she decides to avoid Michael during her stay in this small community.

Finally, they reach a beautiful mansion and estate in the middle of nowhere. There are horses in the pasture and gorgeous green grass with rolling hills which seem to never end. The brick mansion looks welcoming as Precious spies white daylilies, pink irises, and cherry blossoms surrounding the gorgeous structure. Kudzu is wildly growing around the trees and mansion. It takes Precious's breath away as she gazes on this home that has to have cost over thirty million dollars.

Michael drives his tractor up to the front door, gets out, and comes around and opens the door for Precious. "Get out. You're here," he says while watching the expression on her stunned face. Before they can knock on the door, it flies open, and a Native-American woman in a maid's uniform starts scolding Michael for driving his tractor up on the driveway.

"Michael, I've told you at least a thousand times to stop driving that tractor on the pavement. You're going to cost the family thousands of dollars to repave it." She stops when she notices that he is with a woman. She is rather astonished by the appearance of Michael with a woman. The only other woman she has seen Michael with is Rosa, who Michael has loved for what seems like a lifetime. Precious notices the look on the woman's face and files the information away for deeper scrutiny once she has put all the pieces together.

"My name is Precious Jennings, and I have an appointment with Mrs. McBride. My car stopped down the road. I need to call the leasing agent to let him know that I'm having problems with the car. Michael here tells me that I should give him my keys. What do you think?"

The maid studies Precious, searching for what Precious is really asking her. Even though there is dirt on her face and in her hair and her hair is falling down around her face with a faded hairstyle, she can still tell that Precious is a person of elegance.

Finally she smiles at Michael and says, "Michael, you didn't tell her?"

"All she wants to know, Bertha, is if I'm an honorable man—can I be trusted with the keys."

"Well, he has his good days and his bad days. Michael, are you having a good day or a bad day?"

Michael has a scolding look on his face as he says, "I'm having a good day."

Bertha turns to Precious lightheartedly and says, "You heard him, he said he is having a good day."

"Can I trust him with my keys?"

"Yeah, yeah, I think you can trust him." Bertha turns to Michael and makes a face at him. Changing the conversation, she says, "Well, come on in. My name is Bertha. You can use the phone in the hallway."

Precious spies the phone. The phone is between stunning flowers and figurines. Ancestral family photographs in charming frames line the hall walls. Precious makes a mental note to examine the photographs and ask about them later.

As Precious has a conversation with the BMW dealership in Atlanta, she can hear Bertha and Michael engaging in a conversation in the background. The BMW dealer, Philip, who met her at the airport, tells Precious to check a tracking device in the car, and she has to admit that she has no idea what he is talking about. She turns around and Michael is standing in the doorway. She wonders if he would understand what the BMW dealer is talking about. She hates to ask him for any more help, but decides she needs him.

"Michael, could you come here for a second?" She watches as he walks toward her. He walks a little bowlegged, and she must admit that she has never seen a man walk like that before. She concludes that this is the sexiest walk she has ever seen.

"Yeah, what is it?"

"Do you mind talking to Philip for me?"

Michael turns to Bertha and says, "Can you get me a pen and paper?"

Bertha hurries to the drawer underneath the phone and hands them to him. She is about sixty-five years old, and she appears to be fond of the young man she is helping. Michael talks for several minutes, writing down information as he talks, then hangs up the phone.

"Where are your keys?"

Precious takes the keys out of her purse and hands them to Michael without questioning him.

"You can stay here. Bertha will get you something to eat and show you where the shower is. There are extra clothes in the guest room. You can choose clothes there. I'll be back with your car in a few minutes."

Precious asks, "How do you know there are clothes there?"

"Silly little woman, I work here too."

Precious searches Bertha's face, and Bertha says, "Come on upstairs and shower and put on some clean clothes. Then come on downstairs to the kitchen, dear, and I'll get you something to eat. Michael is a good boy, and you don't have anything to worry about." Precious feels a little at ease as she follows Bertha up the amazing spiral staircase.

When Precious finally enters the kitchen, she says to Bertha, "I have never seen anything quite like this before. Drawers and a closet filled with new clothes."

"Mrs. McBride from time to time takes in homeless families— mostly families who have lost their farms. She sets them up with a job and a place to live. She's done this since I've known her, and for that, she has made a lot of lifelong friends."

"Why does she do that?"

"Because she feels obligated to. To whom much is given, much is required."

Bertha takes food from the refrigerator before Precious can stop her. "I would just like a glass of bottled water, please."

"Young lady, I don't mean to talk about you, but you look like you could use something to eat." Precious is happy with her 125-pound frame and wonders what Bertha is talking about. Bertha looks as though she weighs 250 pounds and she stands about five-foot-five.

"I like to keep this weight," Precious says proudly.

"Why?" Bertha replies. She is confused by Precious's answer.

For some reason Bertha reminds Precious of her mother, and she laughs at Bertha's question.

Precious takes a seat at the table and says, "All women want to be this size. I can fit into any style of clothes with this figure. When I start to gain more weight, I just go to the gym and lose the weight."

Bertha turns to her and says, "Have men told you that they like string beans?"

Precious thinks for several minutes and confesses, "No, they haven't, but I know they do."

"How do you know they do?"

"Because they always ask me to go out with them."

"Well, I don't know how they are up north, but men down here like women with a little meat on their bones. I'm going to fix you a sandwich, and I'll give you bottled water to wash the sandwich down."

"Bertha, I don't eat meat."

"Okay. I'll make you a peanut-butter sandwich then."

"Thank you" is all Precious can manage to say while marveling at Bertha's personality. Precious sits up straight and asks, "What is Mrs. McBride like?"

Bertha brings over the sandwich and bottled water and sits next to Precious and watches her eat for a few minutes before she answers.

"Her family has been living down here for generations. Everybody down here is related in some way. I lived on a reservation. I worked at an outpost. When the store closed, Mrs. McBride asked me if I wanted a job. I have a boy and a girl who I haven't seen in ten years. They're ashamed of their heritage. My children are somewhere in the world passing for White, and I have no place in their lives because I don't look White."

Precious is surprised by Bertha's honesty. "What are you going to do when you can no longer work for Mrs. McBride?"

"I'm going to retire off the money Mrs. McBride put in my savings account. Mrs. McBride is taking care of me, and I take real good care of her."

"This must be a special relationship."

"It is. I love her and her family."

"I've heard some horrible things about this town. Please tell me what I should be cautious of."

Bertha debates if she should tell Precious the embarrassing truth about the town. She decides that Precious should know what she is walking into.

"Be careful when you go out, and never go out at night by yourself. Mrs. McBride has gotten some death threats during the past two weeks. People are angry with her and her affiliation with and organization of the Black farmers here. Several people have been beaten up or have come up missing or hung. The Greater New Hope Church and Mt. Carmel Church have been burned to the ground."

"Do they know who did it?"

"No, but we have our suspicions. The mayor and the chief of police, I believe, are in on the whole thing. You can't trust anyone in the town. We can't seem to get them to investigate anything around here."

Precious is quiet for several minutes, then says, "As soon as I take care of my business, I'll be out of this town."

"Well, good for you."

Precious is now at a loss for words because she is concerned about the people she has just met. "I'm sorry for Mrs. McBride, but I know you and others will do everything you can to safeguard her." Precious decides she sounds insincere and changes the topic. "Who is Michael?"

"A special person. Ask him who he is. He'll tell you."

"Where does he live?"

"You know what? I really don't want to talk about people who aren't here. I'll tell you more about Mrs. McBride, though. I have a great deal of respect for her. This is a family raised from generations of slaves, a family that managed to build a farm and raise a family by the Good Book. Along the way, they managed their money well. She and her husband worked hard for everything they have. Everyone in her family has finished college—Mrs. McBride, her deceased husband, and both of her children. One of her children is respected in his field and the other, whom you will meet, is smart but isn't motivated. I believe that this has been a tremendous torture for the poor child. It's got to be hard not living up to your full potential."

Bertha notices that Precious has finished the sandwich and asks if she would like another one.

"No," Precious says. She takes out the address of the cottage she will be staying in and asks, "Do you know where this cottage is?"

Bertha studies the paper. "Yeah. It isn't far from here, just a few miles up the hill." She takes out some paper and a pencil and draws a map to show Precious how to get there. "You know you could stay here."

"Thank you, but I kinda need my own space."

Bertha studies her face and says, "Yeah, I believe that you do, but like I told you before, you better be careful. Mrs. McBride isn't going to understand why a single woman who is in a town full of problems would want to stay by herself. She won't understand why a good-looking woman like you is down here by yourself in the first place."

Precious glances at her watch while helping Bertha clean the kitchen. She washes off the kitchen table and, when she turns around, Michael is standing there with the keys to her car in his hand. "The problem with your car has been fixed. It's outside waiting patiently for you."

Precious smiles and says thanks, then asks, "What do I owe you for helping me? I know you need something for working in the fields all day like you do."

"Sorry, woman, I know you want some of this, but you ain't gonna get it."

Bertha turns around to watch the exchange. She thinks it's all kind of funny. It's been a long time since Michael has joked like that.

Precious says to him, "You must be delusional from being out there in the cornfields too long. What you need is to trade in that tractor for a few counseling sessions. Maybe they can help you firm up your personality." Precious is about to say more, and Michael is about to explode when they both turn to Bertha, who is smiling at the two of them.

Precious walks toward the door and hears someone calling for help.

"Did you hear that?" Precious says to Bertha and Michael.

"Hear what?" Michael asks.

Precious takes a step in the direction of the front door. Her gait is unsteady, and before she realizes it, she faints.

Chapter 7

April 6

Precious wakes up. She is somewhat groggy as she tries to lift her hand and finds that there is an IV attached to it. She tries to sit up and, as her vision clears, she is staring in the face of an attractive, strange older woman wearing a lopsided hat. She tries to wipe her eyes again, and as she does she focuses on Michael, who is standing next to the woman. Bertha is in the room and so is a strange teenager with a Dr. Seuss hat on. Underneath the hat stands a small-framed woman around twenty-one years old who is quite pretty, but the clothes and the hat seem to distract from her beauty.

"Where am I?"

"You're in the hospital." The woman with the lopsided hat sits forward and says, "You did all this just to see me?"

Precious figures that this must be Mrs. McBride, and she is mortified about being laid up in the hospital when she wanted to make a good impression on this woman. All decorum has disappeared.

Mrs. McBride says, "The doctor was just in here, and he said that you have sugar in your blood. Do you eat a lot of sweets, dear? Bertha told me that you don't eat the right foods. The doctor is wondering if you've been hallucinating."

Precious thinks, *This woman has perfect diction and her posture is perfect.*

"Did you hear me? I asked you if you've been hallucinating."

"Well, I … um … I see my mother and sometimes other people from time to time."

Michael whispers to Mrs. McBride, "I called her office this morning, and they told me that her mother and father died recently."

"Poor woman," Mrs. McBride says. "We're going to take you home for a couple of days and nourish you back to good health."

"I can't stay here. I've got to get back home. I just want to show you why you should continue to advertise with our company." This seems pretty silly to Precious, being laid up in the hospital in a hospital gown. Her hair is all over her head, and she is trying to talk to a woman of means about renewing a contract.

"Nonsense. We have plenty of time to talk about that once you're feeling better."

Michael smiles as the others leave the room. He sits comfortably in a chair, staring at the destitute Precious.

"Whatever you do, please don't say anything," she says. "Don't you have the back forty to plow?"

"Nope. I got a field hand working with me today."

"How long have I been in here?"

"Two days. You've been asleep for two days. When was the last time you went to sleep?"

"I can't stay in here. I've got to go."

"Let me see, you can see dead people and phony people, but you can't see yourself?"

"Don't you have a woman somewhere wondering where you are?"

"Nope. I've got time to sit with you."

"You aren't going to make me feel better by being here. As a matter of fact, you're making me sicker."

Michael walks over to the bed and looks into Precious's eyes and says, "Wow, I never noticed before, but you have bloodshot eyes."

"Nurse! Where is the damn emergency button?"

"Okay, I'm going, but I'll be back tomorrow to take you to the McBride mansion."

Several hours later, the doctor returns.

"Young lady, I'm Dr. Smith. You were unconscious when they brought you in and I need some questions answered. Are you Precious Jennings?"

"Yes."

"Who is your next of kin?"

"My sister, Jazzy—I mean Jessica Jennings."

"Would you write her number down please?"

The doctor hands her paper and pencil. The IV is in her right hand, and she is right-handed. She tries to maneuver the pencil in her left hand, but her writing is barely legible.

"I will be your doctor and I've been treating you. I have a few more questions to ask you. Has there been an increase in urination?"

"Yes."

"Have you been excessively thirsty?"

"Why, yes."

"Do you have an increased appetite?"

"No."

"Have you either gained weight or lost weight?"

"I've lost weight."

"Do you have blurred vision?"

"Yes."

"Do you have a skin infection or irritation?"

"Yes. My skin turns red a lot."

"Do you have vaginal infections?"

"Sometimes."

"Miss Jennings, do you exercise?"

"Almost every day."

"Do you eat a lot of sweets?"

"Yes."

"We have run several tests on you. You have borderline Type 2 diabetes mellitus. What that means is your body does not make enough insulin, which is a hormone produced by the pancreas. I'm going to leave several pamphlets with you. When is the last time you've seen a doctor?"

Precious is embarrassed once again. She hasn't had time to make an appointment. "I saw one about a year ago." Precious remembers her family reunions where several of her cousins set up a booth for relatives to get health screenings. Precious was too busy making business deals and didn't go near the booth.

"I spoke with Michael and he says you're a well-educated woman. Don't you know you should have checkups?"

"I haven't had time."

"Then what you are telling me is that you haven't had time to live."

There is a flustered expression on the doctor's face. "The only redeeming quality in this situation is that you exercise. The nutritionist will be in later with a meal planner. I want you to add protein to your diet. I want you to start eating on a regular schedule, and I want you to gain fifteen pounds at least. "

"You want me to gain weight?"

"Yes, I want you to gain weight. You're too small. I'm going to release you tomorrow, and the nurse will set an appointment for you to see me next week."

"Doctor, I plan to be back in Michigan next week."

"Well, give me your doctor's name so that I can share my findings with him."

Precious writes her doctor's name down on the paper.

"I'm not going to give you medicine right now, but I do plan to monitor you while you're in town."

Chapter 8

April 8

Several days later, Precious is still recuperating at Mrs. McBride's home. Her room is large with a deck where she can look out over the rolling hills. She walks out onto the deck and wonders why she never knew that there were Black people who lived like this.

It is noon, and everyone in the house assembles in the dining room to have lunch together. As Precious makes her way to the dining room, she marvels at the inlaid designs on the front door of the enormous mansion. She walks freely through the house with no one asking her where she is going.

Mrs. McBride is sitting at the table waiting for Precious as she walks into the room. The teenager in the Dr. Seuss hat takes her seat at the table too. There is a man that Precious doesn't know sitting with the family. He is introduced to Precious as Dan Lane, a man who owns several grocery stores in the town.

Mrs. McBride and Mr. Lane talk nonstop about the trip to Washington, D.C., that Mrs. McBride will be taking next week.

"These are the papers you need to present to Congress when you go. You shouldn't be going by yourself. Me and several of the men will escort you aboard the plane. I would like to go with you to protect you. Can I go?"

"Someone needs to remain here just in case something happens to me. You have all the information."

"Okay, I'll stay, but if you need me, I'll be there by your side in a hurry."

"I know that, and I thank you for being a good friend."

"I want to be more than just a good friend." Mr. Lane looks back at his notes. "You're going to meet up with representatives from other cities and states. If necessary, we'll march on Washington again to get them to help our farmers."

Wendy, the teenager with the Dr. Seuss hat on, says, "Mom, I'm going with you. It's too dangerous for you to go by yourself."

"Nonsense. You'll go to work next week as usual. I don't want anyone in town knowing what we're doing here."

"Mama, I'm not going to let anybody kill you." She turns to Mr. Lane and says, "She shouldn't be going by herself."

He smiles. "Your mother will be in good hands."

Wendy throws her napkin down. "Then why don't you go?" She leaves the room without saying anything else.

"She's overprotective of me. Trust me, I'll be all right."

"You know, she might be right. You have had some death threats already," says Mr. Lane, who is concerned about her.

"You did forget who I am, didn't you?" Mrs. McBride smiles at the two people remaining at the table.

"Yes, I guess I did, but I'm like your daughter. You shouldn't be going there alone. I don't know what I would do if I lost you," Mr. Lane says, while gazing into Mrs. McBride's eyes.

Precious thinks, *This is much more than I had planned to get myself involved in. These people are in love with each other, and they're about to die for a cause I don't believe in.* Precious stares at the two of them. "Well, I guess I'll excuse myself."

"No, I've got to get back to the store. You stay." Mr. Lane gets up from the table, kisses Mrs. McBride, and leaves.

When he leaves the room, Mrs. McBride turns to Precious. "So why are you down here in the South?"

"I need you to sign a contract. We're giving you the best rates in the company's history."

"What will happen to you once I sign the contract?"

"I'm going home."

"Oh, I see."

"I mean, I believe in what y'all are doing down here, but it has nothing to do with me."

"Young lady, what I'm about to do has everything to do with you. You've spent two days in my home eating the food that Black farmers grew. We are not experimenting with the food that you and your families eat.

"The food we grow is pure. Look at you, up and bouncing around. They want us to sell our food to Third World countries. I don't mind sending food supplies to those countries, but I want to have the right to choose who I do business with."

"Oh, I see," Precious says, deep in contemplation.

"Do you really see?"

"I'm beginning to see. Maybe I did need to eat and maybe I did need to sleep. I see that me becoming a partner in the company that I'm working for is contingent on you signing this contract. You must be a powerful person."

"Well, young lady, I'm not powerful by myself. I have a lot of people backing me. I believe in what I'm doing. Life doesn't mean anything if you aren't doing something that you really believe in."

Precious is beginning to feel her life is linked to this woman as she says, "What do you want me to do?"

"I want you to be careful. You're driving around in an expensive car. People know that you're an outsider, and they may cause trouble for you. I could sign the contract and send you on your way." Mrs. McBride thinks several seconds before she talks again. "I need my attorney to review the contract before I sign."

"How long will that take?"

"I don't know. He's busy working on this current project with me. It might take a couple of weeks."

"Two weeks?"

"Or more."

Precious says, "I'm not trying to rush you, but I would like to get back to Michigan as soon as I can." She thinks more about the extended period of time before the contract will be signed and says, "You know, I think I'm going to spend time at the cottage. I haven't had a vacation in a long time. This hospital trip has reminded me that I need to slow down. I've got too many problems."

"Well, if you do decide to stay, you can stay here."

"No, I need some time to think. Thank you for opening up your home. I believe the fresh food is what helped me regain my health. I do believe that's why I'm feeling so much better. I'd like to take you out to lunch tomorrow. How about it?"

Mrs. McBride straightens up the hat on her head and says, "I would love to join you, but I'm planning a meal at the house tomorrow. You're welcome to join us."

"I just might do that." Precious gets up from the table and says, "I think I'll be going to the cottage today, if you don't mind."

"Well, young lady, I think you're going to be all right. Michael will take you there."

Mrs. McBride rings a bell on the table, and Bertha enters the room. "Tell Michael that the young lady is ready to go to the cottage."

Ten minutes later Michael enters the room. "You're not going to stay here?"

"No. I'm going to the cottage."

"We can't protect you at the cottage."

Precious looks over at Mrs. McBride and says, "I'll be all right."

The two women continue to talk. Michael asks, "Where's Wendy? I'm riding to the cottage with Precious, and Wendy is supposed to follow so that she can give me a ride back."

Bertha says, "She left half an hour ago. She said she had something that she wanted us to see."

Michael goes back into the kitchen and is talking with Bertha. Precious can't make out the conversation and wishes that he would hurry. She would like to finally spend some time alone.

Michael reenters the room and says, "So are you ready to go?"

"Yep. I was ready a long time ago."

Precious hugs Mrs. McBride before she leaves the room and follows Michael outside.

Bertha opens the front door and is about to tell them to be careful when a long black hearse pulls up to the front of the house. Bertha stands there looking at the hearse sitting in the driveway. Bertha is in shock, as the driver does not immediately get out. Both Precious and Michael watch in astonishment when finally a large Dr. Seuss hat appears in the driver's open window.

"Family, like my new car?"

Mrs. McBride walks to the door, staring. She's flabbergasted. "Is this the car that was such a good deal? It's a hearse. Why are you driving this? I know I should have insisted that you go on and get your master's degree."

Mrs. McBride is angry as she walks around the forty-year-old hearse. She wants to say something, but doesn't seem to be able to find the right words to express her anger appropriately. "The backseat is missing. Where are people supposed to ride? I gave you ten thousand dollars. Is this what you spent that money on, Wendy?"

Wendy starts to exit the car while looking at her mother and then motions for Michael to help her out.

Michael says, "I had nothing to do with it. I offered to take you to look at some cars, but your mind was set on this contraption."

"I asked you, where is the money I gave you to go get a car?"

"Well, you see, Mom, that's the beauty of it all. I only paid five thousand dollars for it. I had enough money to buy insurance, and I have enough money to buy a new dress and go to the junkyard and find a backseat. I'll even have money left over. I got a good deal."

"You got a good deal?" Mrs. McBride looks as though she is about to explode as she walks over to her daughter. "I'm not riding to church in that heap of junk. Michael, what do you know about this?"

Michael is defensive as he states, "I told her I would take her to look at cars, and she said, 'When I need you, I'll call.'" Michael talks the way Wendy does, mocking her diction. "She never called."

Wendy walks over to her mother and says, "Don't worry. This is a car that will grow on you, you'll see."

Mrs. McBride throws her hands up in the air and walks back inside the mansion and closes the door. Both Wendy and Michael know what that means. Mrs. McBride is angry.

"Shouldn't we check on her?" Precious asks.

And they both say, "No."

Michael says to Wendy, "Follow us down to Millers Creek, and I'll ride back with you, and we can take the car to Cliff's Auto Shop and see just how much they ripped you off for."

"Why are you going down to that snotty Millers Creek?" Wendy asks Precious.

"I'm going to live there."

"Oh, you're living down in Millers Creek? You must have some money."

Precious gets into the driver's side of her car and says dramatically, "Yeah, I've got a few pennies, and I spend them on worthwhile things."

"What are you talking about?" Wendy walks around to Precious's side of the car.

"That car you bought today is a piece of junk."

"You don't know me well enough to call my car a piece of junk."

Precious turns to Michael and says, "Cowboy, are you coming?"

Wendy stands there staring at this new person and turns to Michael and says, "Who the hell is Cowboy?"

Michael, who is trying not to laugh, tells Wendy to follow him.

Wendy turns back to Precious and says, "You know, you act like a Corsican goat," just loud enough for Precious to hear.

Precious says to Wendy, "Can you come closer to the car? I've got something to tell you."

Wendy approaches the car cautiously. Precious whispers, "I'm not a goat, but you're a French Landrace swine, and you dress like one as well. You should find a better clothing designer."

"Oh, no, you don't, heifa. Michael, I can't stand her already."

Michael smiles and says, "Join the crowd. I'll meet you at Millers Creek."

Precious pulls away from the house and heads out of the circular driveway. Michael points in the direction that Precious should take, then he says, "Do you always have this type of effect on people you've just met?"

"Yep."

They drive for five minutes down a dirt road. Michael then points for her to make a left turn. They pull into a wooded area. One minute after the turn there are beautiful cottages that line a large lake. Precious pulls out a sheet of paper as she continues to drive. "I'm looking for 223 Millers Creek." They drive past several nicely manicured cottages until they finally come to a beautiful ranch-style home with a boat docked at the pier.

An older White man follows her to the home and says, "Are you Precious?"

"Yep."

"Well, your employer has been calling here. He wants to know if you're okay."

Calling people will have to wait, Precious thinks. *That will come after I've taken a shower and rested for a while.*

The hearse pulls up behind Precious's rented BMW.

The White man stands there first looking at Precious, then at the hearse. He finally says, "Did someone die?"

"No," Precious says, then asks, "Can I have the keys, please?"

"I'll take you in. Is this your husband?"

Precious just says, "No."

Wendy gets out of the car and follows them slowly.

The home is decked out in Ethan Allen furniture. A large picture window looks out over the lake. There is a deck, which leads out to a patio with a grill and a picnic table and chairs and with two large lawn chairs.

"My name is Robert Bell. There are several people inquiring about you. People out here have been expecting you."

"What people? No one down here knew I was coming."

"Well, someone knew you were coming because you've been the talk of the cottages."

Precious is a little amazed as she looks up at Michael for support.

Michael says, "You know, you don't have to stay here. You can go on back to the mansion."

Robert Bell, sensing that Precious is concerned about people asking about her, says, "I'm sorry if I upset you. We haven't had any trouble out here for months."

This comment seems to frighten her even more.

She asks, "Have you had trouble here?"

"Yes, but nothing to worry about. You should be safe." Precious thinks several seconds before announcing that she plans to stay at the cottage.

Robert Bell says, "If you have any concerns, you can reach me at this number." He hands Precious a card with his number on it. "I'll bring by the lease tomorrow. You look like you need to rest a bit. You'll be all right."

Precious walks him to the door, and she promises to call if there are any problems.

Michael walks over to the refrigerator, then looks into the cabinets. "Well, you've got a little food here."

"I'm not hungry. I just want to relax."

Michael walks around the cottage, checking every room as he goes.

"What are you looking for?" Precious asks.

"Precious, this is a dangerous town. Robert Bell alluded to it. I can't get you to understand that."

Michael writes down his number and leaves it on the desk. "If you have any problems, call me at this cell phone number."

Precious walks Michael to the door and watches as he and Wendy drive out of sight.

Precious then calls Robert Bell. "Did I get any other phone calls?"

"Yes. Your sister called twice."

"Did anyone else call?"

"Yes. A Philip called twice."

"Did anyone else call?"

"No."

Precious hooks up her laptop computer because she believes that maybe Larry sent her an e-mail.

There are no e-mails from him.

Precious thinks, *I don't understand. I gave him my cell phone number, the cottage phone number, my e-mail, and my web address, and still I haven't heard from him.*

Chapter 9

April 9

Precious stands in front of the large picture window looking out over the small lake while drinking a cup of jasmine tea. She thought several times the night before that someone was trying to break in. Each time she went to check the doors and look around the cottage, there was no one there.

Finally, when she did go to sleep, she slept peacefully and attributes the slumber to finally being at peace. She looks around the room and its design. The kitchen, dining room, and living room are done in an unusual circular design. A hallway leads from the living room back to the master bedroom as well as to another room, which Precious has decided to use as an office. In the middle of the circle are steps that lead to the lower level. In a downstairs room Precious finds a pool table, television, and washer and dryer. Two other rooms seem to be used as additional bedrooms. A sliding door leads to the outside. Precious opens the door and walks out toward the lake. Ducks and geese are playing games in the middle of the lake, and this captures Precious's attention briefly.

A neighbor comes to the back of his porch, and Precious starts to speak when he walks back inside. At a glimpse, she notices that her neighbors are White. She gazes off into a distant field as she watches a tree sway back and forth. The tall oak tree continues to catch her attention, and she feels saddened by this tree.

She stares at the large oak one more time and decides she would much rather walk over to the tree. She passes several cottages before she stands in front of the tree. She searches for any telltale sign of the age and decides that it has to be at least two hundred years old because the tree seems to reach up to heaven. The branches wave back and forth. She decides to sit on the ground, underneath the tree. The wind blows across her face, and she smells nature. She notices that her neighbors are coming to their windows and watching her as she sits there, tears falling from her eyes as she remembers that she has just buried her parents and how all alone she feels at this minute.

Tears continue to flow as she takes in her new environment. *I don't know a soul here.* Precious has no idea how long she'll be here, but has made up her mind that as soon as she can seal this deal, she'll return home to a more familiar environment. She pulls herself up from the ground and notices the tears streaming down her face. *What is going on here?* she thinks as she tries to recover from the aura that seems to surround the tree.

She throws a rock into the lake and watches as the ripples go farther out.

She walks slowly back to her cottage as she watches her neighbors watch her behind their large closed drapes.

Precious makes up her mind that the first phone call will be to Mrs. McBride because she knows that when she calls her boss in Michigan he will want to know if she has started working yet. The phone rings three times before Bertha answers.

"Hi, Bertha. This is Precious."

"Oh, I know who you are. Did you have breakfast yet?"

"Yes. I had some cereal, toast, and one egg. The groundskeeper came by this morning and told me that he and his wife went to the store earlier yesterday and brought a few items for me."

"Well, that's good."

"Is Mrs. McBride available?"

"Yes, she is. She told me if you called, she would like to speak to you."

"Well, I would like to come over for lunch today. She invited me yesterday."

"Just a moment. I'll tell Mrs. McBride that you're on the phone." Several seconds later, a second phone is picked up.

"Young lady, how are you today? Are you feeling better? Are you eating right?"

Precious senses a genuine concern for her health. "I'm better—eating breakfast and resting like I should."

"What would you like for lunch, dear?"

"Mrs. McBride, anything you prepare, I'll eat."

"Well, I'll make sure it's enjoyable and healthy."

Precious hesitates, but then asks, "Have you looked at the contract?"

"No."

"Just checking."

"Sure you were."

"Do you want me to bring anything today?"

"Just your appetite."

Precious says, "See you at noon."

Precious hangs up the phone and feels as though she has just finished a conversation with her mother. She picks up the phone one more time and calls DeVeux Advertising. When she reaches DeVeux's office, his secretary states that he isn't in. Precious breathes a sigh of relief. She really doesn't want to talk to him. There are too many things she'll have to explain that she doesn't have the answers to.

"Please, just tell him that I'm all right and that I'm working on the account. I have a meeting with Mrs. McBride this afternoon. I'll call him back tomorrow to let him know the progress."

Precious thinks, *Why have people called her a difficult woman? I enjoy being in her presence.*

Precious looks through her clothes for just the right outfit to wear and settles on a yellow summer dress and a yellow-and-red hat that matches perfectly. She pulls out her red shoes and her red-and-yellow bag and decides that this will be the right combination. It is ten o'clock, and Precious decides, after sanitizing the bathroom, that she will reward herself with a hot bath. She finishes her bath with a floral perfume she found in Paris last year. She has just finished combing her hair when the doorbell rings. When she peers out of a window, there stand Wendy and Michael with bags in their hands.

Precious slips on a deep green silk robe and marches to the door and answers it quite seductively.

She is surprised that Wendy and Michael are at her house this early in the morning. "Come in," she says.

Michael realizes that coming to Precious's house might not have been such a smart move, but he is concerned about her safety at Millers Creek, so he doesn't mind if she thinks he's being too forward. Michael clears his throat and says, "Bertha asked us to pick up a few things at the store this morning." Michael watches as Precious moves away from the door, and it is difficult for him to take his eyes off her.

"I just talked to her on the phone, and she said nothing about this."

Wendy walks past her and says, "That's the way she is. Michael, can I have this doughnut? You know she ain't going to eat it."

Michael nods as Wendy makes herself comfortable at the kitchen table while rummaging through the bags for other food to complement the pastries she has just brought in.

"Miss Snob, you got any milk?"

Precious walks over to the refrigerator and pulls out the carton of milk she opened earlier and says to Wendy, "Here you go, Raggedy Ann."

Precious looks out in the direction of the oak tree and says, "You see that oak tree over there?" She points to the tree while talking to Michael.

"Yeah, I see it."

"Well, what's the history of this area? I get a really sad feeling about this place."

Michael takes a deep breath and says, "This used to be the lynching and hanging part of the town. Families were dragged out here and hung. I remember being told that a Black man was hung out here because he forgot to say 'yes, sir' to a man. The tree out there has taken a lot of Black folks' lives."

Wendy, Precious, and Michael look soberly at the tree as images fill their minds.

Finally Precious says, "I have a meeting with Mrs. McBride. How can I convince her to sign the contract?"

Wendy looks strangely at Precious. "You treat her with respect. That's how you work with our—"

Michael cuts her off. "She's a stately matriarchal woman who was married to one of the smartest men in the South. They were able to turn his crops into a multimillion-dollar business. Their business is now in jeopardy because the markets are not taking their products."

"Why is Mrs. McBride fighting the government?"

Michael takes a seat at the kitchen table beside Wendy, who is still eating. Finally he says, "For years, Black farmers have not gotten the same kind of help from local Department of Agriculture offices as White farmers have. Pure discrimination. Most of the loan applications for Black farmers have been delayed or turned down. Or approval on a loan to pay for seed for planting crops wouldn't come through until it was too late to plant, making it almost impossible for the farmer to keep up the payments on any loans he already had. And the USDA offices were always quick to start foreclosure proceedings when a farmer didn't pay.

"Finally two Black farmers sued the USDA. Eventually a class-action suit was filed and a settlement was reached, called the Pigford Consent Decree. But there were problems. The farmers didn't have much time to file a claim, so the deadline was extended. Then, even those that did get their claims in have had a hard time getting the money that's due them. Most haven't received a dime. Not one farmer here has seen any of the money."

"Black farmers are being exploited and penalized. And that has to stop. Many are facing certain bankruptcy and loss of their farms and their livelihood. This town wants the farmers bankrupt. Whites here don't want any uppity Black folks in their town. They're glad the Black farmers haven't received the payments the USDA owes them. Now they're going after Mrs. McBride because she's pursuing legal action on behalf of the Black farmers. She's even received death threats."

Michael seems passionate about the issue. He states proudly, "Mrs. McBride is organizing Black farmers in this area so that they'll get their fair share, so they won't be left out. We're having a meeting tomorrow. You're welcome to come if you have time."

Precious thinks about it for several minutes and decides she would like to know more about what is going on.

Chapter 10

April 9

Precious stands in front of the mirror and admires the Christy Meyers dress with its sleek style. Instead of feeling like she's on top of the world, she feels saddened and attributes her mood to the disappearance of Jessica Zellman. She is now wondering if there was anything else she could have done that would have prevented her kidnapping.

She calls her cousin Ryan to find out if he has heard anything. He tells her that there are no leads to Jessica's vanishing into thin air. He tells her that there have been several demonstrations in the city and that most of the people there believe that there is a conspiracy involved in the kidnapping.

Precious then asks him about the rapper DeShan Williams, who disappeared several weeks ago.

"I'm not sure what's happened to him either. I'm concerned about him too. People are saying that he's crazy and that he just walked away from a lucrative contract. I don't believe that. Why would someone walk away from that amount of money? Why wouldn't he tell his family where he was going? There are other people missing too. I don't understand it, but I'm going to keep looking. Are you having fun down there?"

"I like the people here. They're different and dancing to a different moment in time."

"When are you coming home? I'm worried about you."

"It sounds as though I'm going to have to wait until this lady comes back from Washington, D.C., before she'll sign the contract, so it looks as though I'll be here for a while."

"Well, being down there might be a lot better than being here right now. If we don't find Jessica Zellman, there could be riots."

Precious changes the conversation. "Have you heard from Drinking Scott?"

"Yeah. I saw him yesterday in one of his better moods. He's staying closer to home now that he knows that you aren't going to be here to save him. He told me what you did. Don't you have enough to do?"

"Yeah. I want this lady to sign the contract so that I can come home or take a vacation somewhere. Have you heard from my love? He hasn't called me."

"I told you a thousand times to leave that deadbeat wannabe player alone. He was out with the mayor's daughter the other night at a five-hundred-dollar-a-plate dinner. When he saw me there he introduced her as his friend. Leave him alone and find someone who's truly going to care about you, Precious. Aunt Sarah gave you an important name because you're truly precious. You keep cheating yourself with half-a-man Larry. Damn, you're stubborn and fine. How come you're the only one who doesn't know the value of your existence? Larry knows it. That's why he keeps coming back. He'll never find another woman with the sophistication you have. Drop that zero and get yourself a hero."

Precious laughs. "Oh, now you're quoting songs?"

"I do what I have to do to get you to listen to me. He won't come to family events, strings you along, and gets everything he can from you with just idle talk about maybe marrying you. I could go on, but I've got people to find."

"I'm glad you've got people to find, Ryan. I'll talk to you later. I've got to go to a luncheon."

"Well, I kinda know you, Precious. When things get a little too hot, you're ready to ride up out of the conversation, but not to worry. If I have to come down there to shake some sense into you, I will. Have you met any fine women yet?"

"Bye, Ryan. I know I need to work on myself. Thanks for sharing information with me." Precious hangs up the phone, angry that someone in her family has found out about her psychologically abusive relationship. It has now been confirmed, and she is furious that she has allowed herself to be played in this manner.

She pulls the dress up close to her body. She thinks of what her mother said to her about her name. "You have a special gift. Make sure the people you share your gifts with are worthy enough."

Precious stands in front of the mirror. "I deserve more." She pulls the dress closer and admits that she's more than her beautiful shape and her magnificent smile.

Precious gazes at herself one more time, and she is thankful for the four-day trips to the gym and reminds herself that she needs to find a gym fairly soon. She applies her makeup like the Fashion Fair models that she has seen numerous times in the magazines. She then puts on her hat, which serves a dual purpose of keeping the sun out of her eyes and matching her dress perfectly. Precious then chooses the contents she will need today. She pulls out her wallet, comb, cell phone, tissue, and lipstick and places them in her small purse.

She hears someone outside of her cottage, and for an instant she wishes that Michael were still there. She walks slowly to the door and opens it. She then walks outside. There's something not right about the morning air. Even though she can't see danger, she knows that danger has arrived.

Precious goes back into the cottage and searches the room for her attaché case—she has brought two with her. She decides to take the black one. She checks it for contracts, advertising rates, her most expensive pens, a notebook, and her miniature radio-size computer. She decides to throw several tampons in her secret compartment—she can feel the cramps coming on and doesn't want to be surprised in her Christy Meyers dress. She hears another sound outside her window and peeks out, but sees no one.

Precious checks the clock in the living room, and she still has time to see how her stocks are doing. She turns on the all-news station. There is an emergency bulletin, and Precious takes a seat in front of the television to listen.

The commentator says, "We have a late-breaking news story that has the country bracing. Around the country, we have people who have been kidnapped from their homes. The FBI is looking for Richard Wyle, a cattle farmer; Jessica Zellman, an activist from Michigan; and Abu Malik Aziz bin Baaz, who is an economist from New York City. If you know the whereabouts of any of these people, please call 1-800-555-0000 as soon as possible."

Their pictures are being shown on television, and Precious remembers Jessica's face. She sits for several minutes wishing she had someone with whom she could share her feelings.

Precious decides it is time to go talk to Mrs. McBride. It is 11:30, and already it's hot. Precious climbs into her BMW and heads out of Millers Creek. She glances back, and the neighbors are still watching her. *Get a life,* she thinks as she pulls out onto the dirt road. She also thinks, *It's kind of frightening being kidnapped from your home.* She looks out at the tall oak tree and thinks, *In addition to being taken, you can be killed.* She thinks about the woman who told her that she runs pretty, and she believes that the remark was an unintentional criticism of her life. Precious is concerned about what Michael has told her about the people who were killed there. She isn't used to people peeking at her through windows and not speaking.

As she drives down the dirt road, another car follows her from afar. Precious looks into the rearview mirror and notices the car. It looks like the car that followed her on the highway. She has to think fast. As she drives past the acres of farmland, she spots a small store.

She turns into the store's parking lot. The car speeds down the dirt road past her. She sits there for several minutes before deciding to get out of her car. She isn't sure if she should tell someone that she is being followed. She tries to talk herself out of it, thinking, *There must be a million cars like that one. I've been hallucinating. This isn't real either.* She decides to buy bottled water. She checks her makeup in the mirror, then climbs out with the mannerisms of a refined woman.

There in the back of the store she finds a cooler, and she just stands there looking for bottled water and enjoying the coolest spot in the small store. She can hear people talking around her. The men in the store are playing checkers, and there is one man talking about how handsome he is, and the older man who seems to be beating the younger man is asking him if he is so handsome how come he can't keep a woman. The laughter in the place is explosive as Precious brings her drink up to the counter. She can't find bottled water, so she settles for an orange soda.

The men acknowledge her and try to include her in their conversation. Precious has it all figured out. *They'll try to talk to me and get me involved in their conversation, and I'll have to say whether this younger man is handsome or not and then they'll say they haven't seen me around these parts before and then I'll have to tell them why I'm here.*

Precious stands stone-faced behind the man in front of her. She looks out the large window, searching for the car she believes has been following her, but it is nowhere to be found. She glances at her watch and believes she has just enough time to enjoy her drink before she arrives at Mrs. Alexandra Davis McBride's home. Precious can see the mansion from the country store. The laughter continues between the two men. Precious taps her foot with impatience, and for the first time since Precious arrived in the store, they stop talking.

"Well, come on up here," the older man says to Precious. "I'm just passing the time of day here with my nephew."

"How much?" Precious says in her most businesslike voice.

The older man and the nephew study her face, and they both start to laugh.

The older man says, "Girl, you are taking life way too serious. You are too pretty to be that somber."

The younger man starts to act like a preacher when he struts around the room claiming that the drink she has in her hand is going to cause her to go to hell. "I'll tell you why that one drink is going to cause you to go to hell. You see that drink has twelve teaspoons of sugar, and that's too much sugar for the body to process, and eventually it's going to cause you to have sugar diabetes. You're going to be coming back to me asking me to heal you. And I ain't going to do it 'cause I told you in the first place not to drink that drink, but you did it anyway. Can I get an amen?"

The older man says, "Amen."

Precious stands there trying to be serious, but a smile breaks out on her face. The younger man doesn't stop. He lifts his arms in the air and continues, "I can heal you today. I can heal you from all of your sins. All you have to do is give me your phone number, and I'll rock your world from sea to shining sea."

Precious is grateful for the opportunity to laugh. She is able to compose herself as she stops the jovial moment and says, "Well, I'm not going to give you my phone number, and all I want to know is, do you have bottled water."

The young man moves toward the counter, puts one hand on his chin and says, "Right here. You walked right past it. Give me a dollar, sweet thang."

Precious gives him a dollar and twenty-five cents and tells him that the performance was worth the extra money.

"Will you be back?" he asks as Precious walks out of the door. She leaves the store without answering.

She finishes up her drink before getting out of her car in the circular driveway. She listens to the news. It seems that everyone thinks the rapper who is missing is just trying to get out of his contract, and he is somewhere hiding out. Precious thinks, *How come no one thinks this young man has been kidnapped?*

Precious looks around for the notorious tractor, but it is nowhere to be found, and she secretly wishes that Michael could be there for lunch.

Precious mounts the steps to the beautiful mansion. She checks her Movado watch, and she determines that she is two minutes early. After ringing the doorbell once, Bertha opens the door with a smile.

"Hello, Precious. Mrs. McBride is looking forward to your visit today. You look so lovely. I love the hat."

Precious is a little nervous, and she is sure that Bertha knows it. "Thanks so much for the bags of groceries. I appreciate your thoughts for me. I haven't had a chance to go shopping yet, and they'll come in handy tonight. Where would you suggest that I go shopping?"

"Well, there are several places: The two stores on the south side and the others on the east side of town. Mr. Lane owns the two stores on the south side. His stores are where we take some of our fruits and vegetables. You may want to keep that in mind when you go shopping."

Precious nods.

Bertha can tell that she's more interested in talking with Mrs. McBride.

"Come on in the formal dining room. Mrs. McBride is about to have lunch."

Even though Precious has seen the rooms more than ten times, she is still in awe of the exquisite rooms. Precious follows Bertha through the stunningly picturesque home. Precious wishes that she had time to explore the pictures and some of the antique furniture. She makes a mental note that if she's ever invited again that she'll ask if she can explore Mrs. McBride's home.

Precious's breath is taken away by the early nineteenth century Steinway grand piano that sits comfortably in the dining room among flowers and plants. Precious plays several keys, listening to the tuning, then she runs a scale.

Mrs. McBride walks into the room and listens for several seconds before speaking. "So, young lady, do you play the piano or are you just playing with it?"

"I can play. I just haven't played it in a couple of years."

"Would you like to honor us with a couple of ariettas after lunch?"

"I would love to play." Precious is excited as she stares at the piano one more time before leaving it.

Precious watches Mrs. McBride for several seconds. She concludes that her mother would have loved Mrs. McBride. She looks stately in her no-nonsense persona. Mrs. McBride is fashionably dressed. She, too, has on a hat, and her orange dress gives away a spunky personality. She acts as though she is having lunch with a dignitary, and Precious loves the feeling. There is a sparkle in Mrs. McBride's eyes. She gives Precious a half smile.

"Come, my dear. I'm just about to have a cup of tea. Would you like some?"

"Mrs. McBride, with all due respect, I thought this could be a working luncheon."

"So you did? I'm not about to discuss business with you. I want to have one meal where I can just sit back and enjoy the food. Do you enjoy the food you eat?"

Precious says, "Yes, I do."

Mrs. McBride sits forward. "So tell me, exactly how do you enjoy your food?"

Precious thinks, *That is a stupid question.* "I enjoy my food by eating it."

Mrs. McBride puts her hand to her hip and says quietly, "Food should be eaten slowly. You should be savoring every bite that you take. Close your eyes and sip the tea."

Precious sips the tea and really enjoys how it makes her feel. "I would like to know everything there is to know about you today."

"Not yet. There'll be time for that."

Bertha brings in lunch. There is meatloaf, mashed potatoes, summer squash, green beans, and homemade rolls.

Precious thinks, *I'm only eating meat because the doctor told me I needed protein. This is too much food for lunch.*

"Now, young lady, take a bite of food, close your eyes, and chew slowly."

Precious does it, and she can't believe how good the food tastes. She opens her eyes, astonished. Mrs. McBride laughs as she watches the expression on Precious's face.

"I grow these vegetables here on the farm."

Precious confesses, "I've never tasted anything like this."

"Sure, you did," Mrs. McBride says while tasting the meatloaf. "You had the same kind of food yesterday when you visited. I could tell that you weren't enjoying your food. You were moving it around on your plate like you were arranging a business meeting."

After lunch Bertha clears the table and leaves Precious and Mrs. McBride to talk.

"Who was your father?" Mrs. McBride asks.

"He owned several supermarkets in Michigan. They were large stores, and he would help people out when they didn't have money to pay for their groceries."

"What did your mother do?"

"My mother was a nurse. She had a strong personality. She was always taking in children."

"So from our previous conversation, the DeVeux Agency will make you a partner if you can bring in this multimillion-dollar account. Is this correct?"

"Yes, it is, madam. I thought we could go—"

"We will relish the lunch we just had before we have any other discussion, and then I will decide if I want to go over the contract with you." Mrs. McBride sips her tea.

Precious has determined early on that Mrs. McBride is playing a sort of psychological game with her.

"What kind of degree do you have?"

"I have a BA degree in business and an MBA from Harvard University. I had several other jobs before coming to DeVeux Advertising, and I decided that I loved doing this more."

"Oh, I see. And what were those other jobs?"

"I was an accountant at a prestigious Michigan law firm."

"Oh, I see. And what makes you think that you can handle my account?"

"I've done my homework on you. You're listed in the Fortune 500. You're responsible for coordinating the march on Washington. You raised two children alone after your husband died, and you allow your children to be their own person. You're a proud woman, and you expect the people working with you to have a level of professionalism as well as intelligence. You can't stand to have people around you who procrastinate. Your family was the first Southern Black family to become multi-millionaires, and that started with your great-grandparents who bought this house from their slave owners. And if I take this account, I better be good because if I'm not, you wouldn't hesitate to fire me.

"If you allow me to work with your account, I could get your organic products in national magazines and on radio and television. I would design a catchy phase for your products that will make you a household name—not only in this country, but globally as well. "

"Why aren't you married?" Mrs. McBride says without flinching.

"My father was the best, and I haven't found the best yet."

"Oh, I see. Do you think that your mother had a hand in making him the best?"

"Yes, but she had something to work with."

"I would like to hear you play the piano now."

Precious trips over a pillow on the floor while making her way to the piano. She's glad that she doesn't have to answer any more questions, and playing the piano has always brought back fond memories of her playing in her mother's living room for her guests. Sometimes she would sit in the dark and play the piano for Larry, and this was always a prelude to lovemaking.

Precious turns to Mrs. McBride, who has found her way to a chair near the piano while still sipping tea. "Now you are entering my world. I want you to close your eyes and experience every chord that I'm about to play."

The music is melodic, and Precious plays with passion as she remembers the ups and downs of her life, and somehow she is able to encompass this into the music. The time away from the piano only seems like moments. Bertha comes out of the kitchen and sits on a couch. She, too, closes her eyes and allows the chords to transport her to another time and place. The music takes Mrs. McBride's breath away, and she regrets Precious playing her last note.

When all eyes open, there stands Wendy in shock, watching the three women. "Wow, Precious, I didn't know you could play like that. So you do have some talent." Wendy sits down next to her mother.

Suddenly Precious starts another melody and turns to Mrs. McBride as she makes up a rhyme:

> If you advertise with DeVeux you will
>
> Save more money and have fewer bills
>
> While doubling your cash and making greater deals.

Mrs. McBride is stunned as she sits in disbelief. When she finally does speak, she says, "Why did you feel you needed to do that?"

Precious knows right away that playing jingle music was a big mistake.

Wendy starts laughing. "You were so close to getting that contract signed with the way you were playing the piano and then you started playing an advertisement. You are so silly. I can't believe it. You could have been out of here by tomorrow. Now you're going to pay for that blunder." Wendy laughs again as she stares at Precious in disbelief.

Mrs. McBride gives Wendy a reprimanding stare, and Wendy knows that this means to keep quiet and not say another word.

"Young lady," Mrs. McBride says to Precious, "I believe you did that on purpose. Why would you intentionally muddle up a beautiful moment with nonsense? For the life of me, I don't understand your point."

Precious is about to speak when Mrs. McBride starts talking again. "This is what's wrong with individuals. You don't know how to enjoy and savor life. How unfortunate for you."

Mrs. McBride turns to her daughter as Wendy returns from the kitchen with some food.

"When are you going back to college for your master's degree?"

"I'm not. I've been talking to Michael about this patent that I'm working on. It's makeup with all-natural products."

Precious wonders, *Why would she be talking to Cowboy about makeup?*

"Where is Michael now?" Mrs. McBride asks Wendy.

"He went to put gas in the tractor, and then he said he was coming to the house for lunch. Guess what, Mom. Guess what Precious calls Michael."

Precious has been on the hot seat long enough and would rather not have any more attention directed toward her.

"What does she call Michael?"

Wendy smiles as she looks over at Precious, who is shaking her head, begging her not to tell on her, but Wendy isn't listening.

"Well, she calls him Cowboy." Wendy starts laughing.

"Oh, I see. So why is this your business?"

"Everything around here is my business. Everything," Wendy says, asserting her importance in the group.

Michael walks into the room. "I'll just take some grub and sit in the backyard."

Mrs. McBride says, "And why would you be wanting to sit in the backyard? And when did you start calling food grub?"

"'Cause I'm the hired hand."

Wendy starts laughing so hard she spills the teacup next to her. She is glad there is nothing in it.

Mrs. McBride sits up straight. "Since when did you become a hired hand? Must I remind you that you have a Ph.D. in developmental biology in the area of biotechnology? And must I remind you that you quit your job because your superiors were experimenting with the food supply? My son, the unemployed doctor."

Precious does not know which is more shocking, the fact that Mrs. McBride has lost her composure and her hat has almost fallen off her head or the revelation that Michael might be a brilliant man and that he is Mrs. McBride's son.

Michael smiles. Watching his mother's hat fall to the left side of her face and Precious's expression are amusing to him.

"I'm going back to work. I've got the back forty to plow." Michael tips his hat to the women and heads for the door. Precious stops him as he tries to leave.

"I can't believe it."

"You can't believe that Mrs. McBride is my mother?"

"No, I can't believe that you might be smart."

Michael laughs hysterically as he leaves the room.

Chapter 11

April 10

The next morning the sun is rising over the rolling hills as Mrs. McBride walks outside to enjoy the sunrise. She sits there until the sun has made its way over the mountaintop and she claps when the sun finally arrives. She has done this for years. She remembers that it started right after Michael was born. Her reason for praise is she thought she was unable to conceive.

David Eagle Feather comes out of nowhere and pulls up a chair next to Mrs. McBride.

"Sorry I missed the first light this morning."

"Where were you? It was quite a performance, a magnificent sunrise."

"I had to get some things ready for my own show. Is the woman who waits on you here?"

"She doesn't wait on me. She has a job to do, and she does it."

"She cooks your food and washes your clothes."

"You make it sound as though I'm lazy. When I was a younger woman, you know I took care of my own house."

David Eagle Feather doesn't say anything. Even though he has been coming to Mrs. McBride's house for thirty years, she doesn't know anything about him. She doesn't know where he lives, if he's married, or whether he has children. When she asks him about anything personal, he just gives a confusing answer. He never takes anything from her and never asks for anything. Sometimes he brings her fruits and vegetables, and they enjoy them for breakfast.

Mrs. McBride has asked Bertha about him, and Bertha knows little about him either. She does know that he has been called a chief by other people in the Native-American community.

Finally Mrs. McBride says, "Yes, she's still in bed. Would you like me to prepare breakfast for you this morning?"

"No. I had breakfast already."

Nothing is said for several minutes as they both listen to the sounds of nature. Finally David Eagle Feather walks into the house and out of sight.

This is the day that Mrs. McBride is to make a speech to the Black farmers, and she thinks about what she might say.

She sees Precious drive up slowly and park her car.

"Good morning, Mrs. McBride."

"Good morning, young lady. How did you sleep?"

"I slept fine, but I got a note on my door this morning."

"What did it say?"

Precious removes the note from her pants pocket. Her hands are shaking as she reads it. "It says, 'Get out of here or die you nigger.'"

"Michael will help you move."

"I'm sorry, Mrs. McBride. I'm not moving just because someone wrote me a note."

"Precious, you don't understand. You're not safe there. Listen to me. I can't protect you there. Move into the house. I have a guesthouse in the back by the pool. You may have that if you wish."

David Eagle Feather walks out of the house. Precious is a little frightened by his appearance. The sight of him sends chills down her spine, and she doesn't know why he is having this effect on her. He has on a ragged shirt with one feather hanging on a band around his head.

"I must get back to work. I don't have a lot of time to finish my work," he tells Mrs. McBride.

"What kind of work are you doing?" she asks.

"The work of life."

Mrs. McBride is confused by his words, but says to him, "This is Precious. She's here to do business with me. She got a note this morning when she woke up."

"Good morning, madam. Let's see your note." David Eagle Feather reads the note and gives it back to Precious. "Where do you live?"

"Millers Creek."

David Eagle Feather walks away and is almost across the hill when he abruptly turns around and says, "Move." He then walks out over the hills and disappears from sight.

"Young lady, are you here because you're going to the meeting with me this morning or do you have another jingle you want me to hear?"

"I'm sorry about yesterday, and yes, I came to give you my support."

"Well, we're going to take my automobile." Mrs. McBride inspects the daylilies growing in her garden before heading toward the garage. There inside is a ten-year-old black Cadillac in mint condition. Precious walks around the car before she concludes that this vehicle is in such good condition that it could easily take them both around the country without even an oil change.

Mrs. McBride starts the car, then turns on the radio, searching for the farm reports. She does not back out of the garage until she hears the report. She then searches for classical music as she heads down the dirt road.

"How come you don't ask the town to pave the street?"

"Because then there would be a lot of cars coming this way. I don't care for traffic."

Mrs. McBride slides her shoulder to the side of the door. Her hat is tilted to the side just like the young people Precious has seen in Detroit while they are driving their vehicles ever so coolly. Mrs. McBride drives with one hand as she talks to Precious. "You do not understand the people here. It isn't safe for you to live in the cottage."

"Well, I can handle myself. I've seen danger before. Just because some ignorant person writes an ignorant note, it isn't going to stop me from living wherever I want to live."

"Well, I could force you to move."

"And how would you do that?"

"I could hold the contract over your head. I don't know what world you live in, but this note is dangerous in the South."

"Mrs. McBride, I don't mean to be disrespectful to you. I know you're looking out for my best interest, but I truly can handle myself. I remember several months ago when a client tried to force me into a compromising position."

"What did you do?"

"I went to his general manager and I told him what he did."

"What happened?"

"He was fired."

"Who are you going to tell about this note?"

"I'm going to the mayor."

"Let's say that you have time to go to the mayor. What do you think he's going to do about it?"

"He as well as the police will help me."

"What if you can't trust them?"

"I'll go as high as I need to go."

"Precious, I'm worried about you. You don't seem to understand the gravity of your situation. You've got to wake up, and you've got to wake up real soon."

"Well, if I have any more problems, I'll move into your guesthouse. I promise."

"Oh, I see."

"I'm drawn to something down here. There's something that I'm supposed to learn, and I'm not letting any hateful person send me a note telling me that I'm not supposed to be here, that I'm not supposed to be anywhere. If that would be the case, anyone in my past or future could write me a derogatory letter and I would take off in flight. I just won't do it. I won't run away."

"Well, all of that seems courageous, but if you're fighting battles alone, it doesn't seem practical to risk your life and have people who care about you upset and wondering how you are. It just doesn't seem right to me."

Mrs. McBride is still puzzled by Precious's statement as she drives down the narrow dirt road, heading toward the downtown area.

They pass several people who wave as they lean up against their fences talking to their next-door neighbor.

They finally reach Crossword High School. Mrs. McBride pulls into the football field, where there are at least a hundred cars parked in the lot. The stands are filled with Black farmers. Even though it rained the night before, the weather has gotten hot. Precious seems a little surprised that there are so many people who are out to hear Mrs. McBride. For a moment, it appears that the entire population of Star is there. Precious wonders how Mrs. McBride was able to get so many people out to listen to her talk.

Mrs. McBride straightens up her hat one last time as she exits the car.

"You can sit up there in the stands. This won't take too long."

Precious starts to walk toward the stands. The rain has made gigantic mud puddles, and Precious tries to jump over them as she walks. She happens to look up just in time to witness the entrance of Michael in his Buick truck. She looks over at the crowd, realizing that she doesn't know anyone. She decides to wait for Michael. Precious watches as he makes his way toward her. Even though Michael doesn't look like gold, he carries an air of royalty like an African prince of Swaziland. *Man, Precious thinks, this man is so fine and on top of it. He's intelligent too.*

Michael speaks first. "Are we still fighting?"

"Yes. You are an imposter."

"I am not. When you saw me on my tractor, that's really who I am."

"You know what? You told me in the hospital that I wasn't real. Well, you ain't either."

Michael waves at several people and stops to whisper to Precious, "You listen here, missy, I've got a letter of honor from my mother and an endorsement from my sister Wendy who thinks I'm really cool. You can't beat that."

Precious realizes that she's being too serious. She expected Michael to tell her something that would make sense to her. She decides to continue the lighthearted discussion. "It's been raining. Aren't you going to lay your coat in the puddle so that I can walk on it and not get my feet wet?"

"Why don't I just pick you up and put you over my shoulder and carry you like a sack of flour?"

This gets Precious laughing for the first time today. "You can't carry me. I'm too heavy."

"Lady, please, you need some meat on those poor brittle bones of yours."

"Men like my small frame."

"I don't. You need to eat a sack of potatoes. I have some in the back of my truck."

"What, are you scared there's going to be a famine and you got a sack of potatoes just in case there is one?"

Michael smiles. "I always come prepared."

They both laugh as they walk toward the stands. When Michael starts walking next to her, she says, "I might be able to drum up more business with the people here today."

Michael assists her as she tries to jump over another puddle.

"I believe that it would serve a purpose if I could convince people to advertise with my agency. You know these people, don't you?"

"Yeah, I know them, but I don't think that's where their minds are today."

Michael takes his time and explains to her exactly what's going on. "If these people don't get the money the government promised them, they're going to starve to death. Can you imagine working all your life for something that you believe in and then being told we don't need your business anymore, stop growing food? You, Precious, were back on your feet again after two days. It's because of the food being grown here. There are so many people dying now because of the food they're eating. Food is unhealthy. So their minds right now aren't into how they can spend money they don't have."

Precious brushes off dirt that has collected around her shoes, then she says, "How do you know so much about it? I thought you were a biologist."

Michael is patient with her comment and explains, "Precious, everything that pertains to anything in this world is related to food and water in some way. If these farmers stop farming, we're going to be eating genetically engineered food being readied for the commercial market, and no one is scrutinizing this food source. It could be generations before we see the extensive damages to mankind. These people here, you can trust their farming techniques 'cause these people have been farming for generations. Nutritionists tell people every day to eat vegetables and fruits. Who do you think is growing them?"

Michael starts to say something else but realizes that he's becoming emotional about the situation. He walks up the bleachers behind Precious, helping her up each step.

He waves at people as he continues to climb to the top of the bleachers. Precious is leading him up to the top bleacher while keeping her dignity and her hair in place as she mounts every step, praying that she doesn't fall between the steps where there is nothing but the ground beneath.

When she finally reaches an open spot, Michael sits down next to her.

Mr. Lane walks up to the podium and says, "Testing. Can everyone hear me?"

The people in the stands start clapping and he goes on. "This past week Mrs. McBride's life was threatened four times. She is a valiant woman who believes in her mission. She will be going to Washington next week to meet with Congress. Today our organizer, Mrs. McBride, will share with you, for a few minutes, what she plans to say. I would like to introduce to you our leader, Mrs. Alexandra Davis McBride.

There is a standing ovation as she mounts the stairs and steps to the podium. She seems to be in charge and in control as she starts to speak. Precious tries to search her face but is unable to read her body language. What Precious does observe is that everyone in the stands stops talking. They pay close attention as they wait to hear what she is about to say.

Mrs. McBride begins her speech. She holds her head up high as she recognizes that she is addressing her most distinguished guests.

"I am here to talk about the plight of the farming industry. My heart goes out to each and every one of you today. We are all invested in this plight. Some of you are losing your farms, while others fear they might lose them. I was told today that none of the farmers in this area have been paid from the Pigford Consent Decree. For those of you who have not gotten paid, I am speaking to you today.

"I will be going to Washington next week to demand that something be done. Someone from the Black farmers should be on the committee with the Secretary of Agriculture to provide our input into the directions of farming. Right now they have two representatives. I will recommend that three farmers from our coalition be allowed to be on the committee to decide when, where, and how the money will be disbursed. We are also interviewing new attorneys who will have our best interests at heart and not sell us down the river for thirteen silver pieces. We will not be exploited anymore. We are tired of people using our pain to advance their own political careers and line their pockets. We will continue to stand up and fight for the rights of every farmer in this country. I will go to Washington standing up for you."

People are standing up clapping as Mrs. McBride reaches an enthusiastic pitch.

"I conclude on behalf of the members of this organization and myself, our specific goals and concerns are debt relief, the ability to file for and get relief."

From the crowd someone says, "What if you lose?"

"First of all, I don't believe I'm going to lose. I would never start something thinking that I'm going to lose. But let's just say that if we do lose, everyone in the world loses, not just us. Unhealthy food will be in the marketplace, and it will continue to produce unhealthy people.

"My son has a Ph.D. in biology. I would like for him to tell you what he has found. Come on up, Michael."

Michael is a little nervous as he walks down onto the field. He doesn't know what he is going to say. He pauses like his mother did as he looks around the bleachers, at the farmers sitting on the benches. He looks into the eyes of people who have worked hard all their lives. He understands the faith they have in believing that everything is going to turn out all right and knows how many of them are only scraping pennies together to keep their farms afloat.

He then looks at Precious for confidence. He turns and stares at the farmers again, noting that when he was a child he attended Sunday school and church with many of the people anticipating what he might say.

He knows that when the words escape his tongue that they will all recognize his Southern accent—he is proud of that drawl. He remembers when he first started out on speaking engagements how the firm for which he had once worked sent him home with a tape recording of the proper pronunciation of words. Michael resented the fact that they couldn't accept him for who he really was. He was a valedictorian in college. He was a capable person in his field of study, and by most he was thought of as an expert in his field, yet the stability for him in the company was contingent on how well he was able to articulate his words. He remembers going to meetings, and people he was talking to were not interested in his research findings, which were pretty profound. They were more interested in how he conjugated verbs and nouns.

Michael learned the art of including his early years on the farm in his speeches. He would talk about the importance of planting good seeds and would weave that into his speeches. This was above and beyond his Stanford education. It also helped that his good looks were enough to mesmerize people who were listening to him.

Yet Michael ponders the direction of his speech. Finally he says, with a Southern drawl, "Hello, my name is Michael, and many of you know me. I've been working in the biotech field and have been away from home for such a long time. It's good to be back. Well, I'm glad to stand before you today to let you know some of the areas we have been working in."

Four cars pull into the parking lot. They make so much noise that everyone's attention is distracted for several minutes. Michael doesn't wait for the participants to exit their cars—he continues to speak—and eventually everyone turns back to listen to what he has to say.

Ten of the meanest White men in the county stand next to their cars as they listen intently to what is being said. Michael is familiar with several of them and knows that they are a part of the Knights of Darkness. Now he has extra pressure—should he tell the truth or should he wait until another time?

"I want to tell you what has been happening in Alabama since 1996. The cotton crops have been genetically engineered to kill insects. It was considered the first crop that has the commercial use of split genes. I guess you are wondering what this has to do with you. Biologists are now working with tissue cultures in agricultural. Instead of farming outside, they are looking to bring products inside. Vanilla has been produced in laboratories, and most of us will be buying vanilla ice cream when we leave this meeting today.

"The rest of the country is not joining in on this fight. If they take down the Black farmer today, they will be coming after White farmers tomorrow. The food we eat will be farmed in Asia, and they will be using pesticides on the food, and who knows what pesticides they will be using and what effects they will have on our health? Let me reiterate, once they have destroyed the Black farmers, they will be going after other farmers. Keep the faith, and if we stick together on this, it will be hard for them to destroy us. Thank you."

Michael starts walking toward the bleachers and is stopped by the men.

"You one of them smart niggers, aren't you?"

"Yep," Michael says.

"Let's see how smart you are when you have to learn to talk again."

"Yeah, let's see," is all Michael says.

Twenty Black men stand like warriors, ready to take a defensive action.

One yells out, "Michael, do you need help?"

The White men move toward their cars. "We'll see you again by yourself. We'll see how smart you are."

They get into their cars and take off down the dirt road.

Precious has heard about overt racism, but had not witnessed it up close. She walks toward Michael, but she isn't alone. Several Southern women are eager to show him that they care too.

Chapter 12

Michael walks Mrs. McBride and Precious to their car.

"I'll be right behind you," Michael says as he closes the door for his mother.

"Michael, I want you to be careful. Those boys aren't playing. I want you to find another job in another city. These people here will never let you live in peace."

"I'm not going anywhere."

"Listen to your mother, Michael," Precious says. "I heard about these men down here. You better pay attention."

Mrs. McBride turns to Precious and says, "Did you hear what you just said?"

Precious ignores Mrs. McBride. "Michael, don't be stupid."

Michael reaches in the open window and locks the door. "I'll meet you back at the house."

Mrs. McBride drives down the dusty dirt road, not saying a word. Precious stares out the window nervously. She has heard about the heinous acts done to Black men. She now wonders if those same acts might be done to her. For the first time, Precious wonders if she should move into the McBride guesthouse.

Precious glances at the worried expression on Mrs. McBride's face.

She has seen that expression before on her own mother's face when she worried about her children and their time of trouble. Mrs. McBride is worried about her son and Precious as well.

Mrs. McBride continues to drive with her hat tilted to the side of her head. "I've given the contract to my attorneys. As soon as they've acknowledged that the contract is adequate, I'll sign it and you can be on your way back to the North."

"Would you like some ice cream?" Precious says, going between celebration and disappointment.

"Yes, I would. Dan Lane owes me money anyway. I'll stop by his store."

It only takes two minutes going down dusty back roads before Mrs. McBride and Precious reach one of the largest stores in the town. In front of the store two men are playing chess and a third man is leaning back in his chair with a straw hanging from his mouth. People are hurrying around them, and the men seem as if they are a fundamental part of the store.

The men come to attention as Mrs. McBride passes by them and says, "If you want a job, I got plenty of work on the farm to do."

One man takes off his hat and says, "We'll do just that, Mrs. McBride," as they start to resume their game.

Inside is a store right out of the Old West. Even though the store is air-conditioned, barrels line a wooden floor that looks as though it has been well taken care of. Precious glances inside the barrels and finds sugar, flour, and spices with large scoops in them. The store is well organized and clean. Fabrics to make beautiful dresses are in one corner of the huge store. Precious has never seen prettier material, and she walks toward it, touching and moving her hand over each fabric as she walks past them.

"Can you sew?" Mrs. McBride asks Precious.

Precious can tell that Mrs. McBride would buy material for her with just a yes answer to the question.

Precious smiles and says, "My mother had a Singer sewing machine, and sometimes she would sew until way after the midnight hour. I used to sit there and watch her, but no, I can't sew. I just haven't had the time to learn to sew like that."

"Well, come on, step away from the material. I'll buy you an ice-cream cone. We'll go sit out in the countryside and you can tell me what your plans are when you finally get back home to your life."

Precious says, "I'll step away from the material and let you buy me ice cream as long as it isn't vanilla."

Both women chuckle as they walk toward the store's ice-cream parlor.

Precious wants to tell Mrs. McBride that there are too many sad memories back in her hometown and she truly likes living in the South much better. The people she has met are much more friendly than many of the people she has known a lifetime in the North. But she remembers the real reason that she's here and her professionalism kicks into high gear. "And I would like to talk shop with you," Precious says.

Mr. Lane enters the room from behind a door. He acknowledges the women with a smile before directing his attention to Mrs. McBride. "Good speech today. Are you ready to go to Washington?" His white sandy hair is neatly combed, and the rays of the Mississippi sun haven't affected his beautiful dark skin.

Mrs. McBride straightens up her hat as she says, "Thanks. I just hope they're ready to listen this time. Do you have the money?"

"And what money would that be?"

Mrs. McBride is a little surprised, but keeps on talking. "Dan, you know that I'm going to Washington. I told you that at the meeting today. You do want me to represent you, don't you?"

"Yeah, my dear. I was just kidding with you. Why are you always so serious?" He leans over the counter and is face to face with Mrs. McBride. "I can't think of anyone better to represent us. How much do you want? Would a thousand dollars cover your trip?"

Mrs. McBride starts to blush. "Dan, you know that people are only giving me a hundred dollars apiece. A thousand is too much."

He pulls out his checkbook. "If you have any problems with anyone, please let me know. I'll pay their share. What you're going to Washington to do is serious business. As I told you before, if I can get someone to watch my shop, I sure would like to go with you, be your protector."

He starts writing the check as Mrs. McBride, once again, is fixing her hat.

"I can take care of myself. I've been taking care of myself, and I've been doing a good job, and I don't need you."

"Yes, you do. You need me. I'll always be there for you too."

He finishes writing the check and hands it to Mrs. McBride. She slides it into her neatly organized purse.

"We would like some ice cream," she calmly says. "What kind would you like, Precious?"

"I would like strawberry."

Mr. Lane says, "One strawberry and one old-fashioned chocolate."

The ice cream starts to melt before they are out of the store.

"Come on. Let me show you something." The women walk down the dusty street. Boards serve as a sidewalk for two blocks, and then there is just a dirt road.

"My husband and I used to take trips all over the world. I got a chance to see how other people were living. I was horrified when I went to Third World countries, and even some countries in Europe were just as bad. My husband and I started producing larger crops so that we could send food to those countries. Every year I get thank-you letters from the governments there. Michael will pick up where we left off.

"He attended Stanford. He spoke at some of the most prestigious colleges and universities in the country, but then he found out that companies were selling genetically engineered food and weren't telling people about it.

"He finally broke his silence at his awards ceremony in Washington. It surprised his colleagues. The press picked up the news, and my son was ushered out of town so fast he hardly had enough time to pack. He has gotten other offers but nothing that will challenge his intellect. You can be at the top of your game one day, and the next day people are petrified to be seen talking to you. My son did make one mistake though."

"What was that?" Precious is curious to find out.

"He married the most mentally unhealthy and unstable woman I have ever seen. I still wonder why he did that. I know that he is still in love with her. She calls at least once a week."

"Where is she?"

"They divorced and he moved back from California. Are you interested in my son?"

"No. He seems nice, but my heart is in Michigan."

Before they realize it, both women are standing at the top of a hill.

"Tell me about him." Mrs. McBride takes a blanket from her bag and spreads it out.

"Well, he is well established in his company, and when we're together, he makes me feel special."

"Do you love him?"

Precious lies and says, "Yes."

"How many times has he called you since you've been here?"

Precious is uncomfortable with the question. "He hasn't called, but just because he hasn't doesn't mean he doesn't love me."

"Precious, your car stopped in a foreign part of the country. You have gotten a threatening note. You've been in the hospital. And you've been gone for almost two weeks. Don't you think it strange that you haven't heard from him?"

Precious thinks, *And yet Michael has been here for me.*

"My husband owned all of this." They look out over some of the richest countryside Precious has ever seen. There is a stream flowing through green meadowlands. "This will all belong to my son one day." It seems to be hundreds of acres of land, stretching on endlessly.

"Precious, let me tell you why I'm giving you this account. You're an honest woman. You came down here and you didn't try to kiss my butt to get what you wanted. Every single time your company sent someone down here, they were always kissing up to me. If all goes well, I'll sign the contract when I return from Washington, and you can be on your way back to this man of yours. But I wouldn't let him get away with how he has treated you since you've been here.

"Everyone that has come down here has acted like they were looking down on Mississippi. The fact is if it hadn't been for a Mississippi or a state like this in the South, most of y'all wouldn't be having the jobs you so much enjoy today. I love the fact that you and I can relate to each other. In many ways we're alike, so see, you can have the account."

Precious gets up and twirls around several times as she says, "I wonder what heaven is like."

Precious helps Mrs. McBride up and Mrs. McBride responds, "I believe it's a beautiful place. My husband is there waiting on me."

Precious says without thinking, "I wonder if heaven could be here."

"Why, yes, Precious, you and I are colliding heavens."

Precious should be happy, but she isn't. This means that shortly she will have to pack up her life and move back to a city where she now feels she doesn't belong anymore.

Chapter 13

April 20

Mrs. McBride is sitting on her porch waiting for the sun to rise. David Eagle Feather joins her and pulls a chair around to the side of the porch and waits for the sun to emerge. Mrs. McBride doesn't acknowledge him right away.

She finally says, "You've been acting awfully strange for several weeks."

David Eagle Feather has a way of asking questions that will keep others out of his affairs. "So you think I am acting strange, do you?"

Mrs. McBride is on to his game and smiles silently because she knows he will not tell her what she wants to know.

"My people used to own this land."

Mrs. McBride thinks, *Here we go again. I've heard this story for almost thirty years now.*

"We could walk freely over this land. Now in less than three hundred years the land is near destruction."

Mrs. McBride says, "I've watched you for years. You and your people just let others run over you, and when the heat gets too hot, you just change your skin color and say that you're White. You never really do anything but sit here on my porch and grumble. I've gotten death threats…. The town that my family helped build I am no longer welcome in. We're not getting a fair price for our products, and then we're getting defrauded out of money that belongs to us. I'm going to Washington tomorrow, and I'll be treated like a sub-human being even though I have more money in the bank than most of the people I'll be talking to. So if I hear one more story about how this land used to be yours and you aren't doing anything about it, I'm just liable to explode right here on my porch."

The sun makes its way over the hills, and Mrs. McBride claps and David Eagle Feather goes into a chant. Mrs. McBride waits until he is finished.

David Eagle Feather walks off the porch. Mrs. McBride waits for him to say something in response to what she has just said. Nothing is said and she watches as he goes over the hills and disappears from sight.

Chapter 14

April 21

Precious sits on her porch, enjoying the early morning ambiance. She isn't concerned about the intimidating note she received. *This is a beautiful place,* she thinks as she looks out over the small lake.

She will be going over to Mrs. McBride's house to see her off to Washington today. Precious glances at the clock and decides to spend a few more moments looking out over the lake before getting dressed to go to Mrs. McBride's house. Precious smiles when she thinks about Mrs. McBride.

There is a knock at the door.

When Precious opens the door, there stand two White men.

"May we come in?"

Precious has an uneasy feeling about the two men, but allows them to come in anyway. Precious opens the door wide and they enter the room. "Have a seat." Precious has on a lounging gown. It is beautiful on her. She asks, "Would you like a cup of coffee?"

"Yes, I think I would," one of them says, and then the other man says, "I would be delighted."

Precious brings them both cups of hot coffee. "Now," Precious says, "who are you and why are you here?"

Richard speaks up first, "You can just call us privates in the war of life. We heard you got a letter yesterday."

Precious takes a seat. "Yes, I did. More of a note, actually."

The other man, Calvin, says, "We live right there." They point to two cottages, one on each side of Precious.

Richard smiles and says, "We just want you to know that we all don't feel that way. If our families can help you in any way, we will."

"I didn't tell anyone around here. How did you find out?"

Both men are uncomfortable as they squirm in their seats, searching for the right answer.

Calvin says, "We heard from several people here that you got the letter."

Precious drills them like a general. "Was it one of the people who sent me the note that you got the information from?"

Richard says, "I'm not sure, but there's a rumor going around out here that you got one."

Precious is getting a little anxious and says, "How come your wives didn't come over? I've been here for two weeks and nobody's been over to welcome me, and now that I get a note you men come over. I don't understand that."

Richard, who seems to be answering most of the questions, says, "We talked to the caretaker, and he told us that you weren't going to be down here long. We thought you just wanted your privacy."

Precious smiles. "I do and thank you for coming over."

Richard replies, "Our wives would like to invite you to a barbecue tomorrow night. Would you like to come?"

Precious thinks, *Am I going to be the barbecue?*

"Thank you so much, but I have plans. I would like to meet your wives though."

Both men get up and hand her their empty cups. Finally Richard says, "We'll let them know you would like to meet them, and we won't take no for an answer."

"I look forward to meeting your wives, and I'll think about the barbecue."

After they leave, Precious hurries and gets dressed and is over to Mrs. McBride's house in a flash.

When Precious gets to Mrs. McBride's house, she finds her on the porch swatting away flies. She swings back and forth on the ebony wooden swing.

Mrs. McBride says, "Would you like some iced tea?" She has on a purple African garb with a beautiful headdress.

"Aren't you going to Washington today?"

"The plane leaves at six o'clock tonight. I have plenty of time."

"Wow, you look so pretty. Yes, I would love some tea."

Mrs. McBride buzzes the intercom and says in a rather stately manner, "Bring two glasses of tea to the Florida room immediately." She turns to Precious and says, "Please come and let me show you some unusual plants I picked up in Kenya several years ago." Precious follows her. Mrs. McBride goes into the house once again to a room that Precious has yet to see.

"Aw, this is such a beautiful room," Precious says, looking around. The room is creatively decorated with a large slave ship, which stands four feet tall in one corner. On the walls are African masks along with pictures that tell the story of the middle passage. On another wall there is artwork of people picking cotton. Fourteen pictures tell the heart-wrenching stories of Black people not having any voices to tell their own story. On another wall are the riches that Mrs. McBride collected from artist Ralph Ashford.

The floors have woven tapestries of women carrying jars on their heads. Handmade baskets fill the room. Mrs. McBride lights several candles as they take a seat close to each other to talk about the symbolisms in the room. As they discuss the characters on the floor, Mrs.

McBride says, "The jars on the women's heads are the world. We are carrying the world on our heads."

"How so?"

Mrs. McBride turns to give Precious a long look. Precious cannot decipher it.

"The world is dependent on women. If the woman in the family doesn't stand up and be the woman that she was meant to be, it's possible that the whole family as well as society will continue to be dysfunctional. Women have got to reclaim their role in this world."

They sip their tea quietly while enjoying the art in the room.

There is a commotion in the house that is disquieting to both women. They jump up instinctively and rush to where the sounds are coming from.

There, slumped over the kitchen sink, is Michael, his face badly beaten and his clothes torn off, revealing bruises and blood.

"My God, what happened to you?" Mrs. McBride rushes over to him, and she holds him in her arms. Precious pulls a cloth off the front of the cabinet while reaching for the phone. She dials 911, then wets the towel. She fumbles with the address as she tells the operator to hurry. She gives Mrs. McBride the towel as she searches for more.

"I was at the restaurant having breakfast with Matt and the boys. I was on my way home and my truck was pushed off the road. I got out and was beaten up by three men who had black sheets on their faces. They told me that if you went to Washing—" Michael falls to the floor, blood flowing everywhere.

Dr. Smith steps out into the hallway where Mrs. McBride, Bertha, Wendy, and Precious are standing. They have been waiting for hours.

"Mrs. McBride, your son is going to be all right. He has two broken ribs and a fractured skull. We're going to keep him a couple of days, at least, to make sure that there isn't anything we've missed. You and your family might as well go home because I have him sedated. He won't be waking up anytime soon."

Chapter 15

Mrs. McBride walks into the house and, with the help of Bertha, she goes up the stairs. Once in her room she thanks Bertha and closes the door. She begins to pack her clothes for the week's journey she has to take. Everything is in place and ready to go. The clothes she will be wearing are hanging on a dress support in her room. She circles the room several times before coming to her realization.

She finally picks up her phone and calls Dan Lane.

"Dan, I can't go today. My son was beaten up. I need you to go. I'll send my daughter over to work in your store while you're gone." She waits impatiently for him to answer.

"What happened to Michael?"

"He was beaten up."

"How is he?"

"He's going to be all right. I just need to be here with him."

"How long will I be there?"

"A week."

"Have you made all the arrangements?"

"Yes. The plane leaves tonight at six o'clock."

"Do you know who did it?"

"No, we don't, and I don't think we're going to find out either."

"I'm going to call and cancel the flight out tonight and reschedule for tomorrow afternoon. We can talk about what happened when I get there. You can also fill me in on the strategy on what I need to do when I get to Washington."

"Thank you, Dan."

"Sure. When I come back and your son is all right, maybe you and I can go out on the town."

"Maybe."

Chapter 16

April 22

Precious goes out to the large oak tree. The branches swing back and forth as though the people who last breathed on the tree are trying to tell her something. She bows down and says a prayer for Michael. After finishing, she just sits under the tree thinking, *What did Cowboy or Mrs. McBride do to deserve what has happened to them?* She spent the morning at the hospital and cried as she touched the bandages on Michael's head. She feels as though she has to protect him and his family. If it hadn't been for the nursing staff who told her she had to go home, she would have been up there all day. Precious questions the nursing staff, wondering how safe the hospital is for Michael. They assure her that no one who isn't on their list of visitors will be able to see him.

There she sits underneath the tree, thinking about the note she received and the guests at her home. She makes up her mind that she doesn't care how bad it gets, she won't leave until she feels the time is right to move on. Precious thinks, *I don't know why this tree is drawing me near. Whatever the reason, I'll follow the directions it has for me.*

She walks slowly back into the cottage. She has made this house her home, putting throw rugs on the hardwood floors, snapping pictures and hanging them above the fireplace and in the dining room. Her own special touches are in the kitchen with a rack to hold the cleaning supplies and dishtowels that match the colors in the kitchen.

The phone rings, and when Precious says hello, the voice on the other end of the phone asks, "How are you, and when are you coming home?"

Precious thinks, *It's Larry,* and she thinks about what her cousin Ryan and Mrs. McBride have said about him.

"Hello, Larry. Why did it take you so long to call me?"

"I've been in the middle of negotiations with a potential client. I miss you, and I was thinking about coming down there."

Precious says, "Please hold on. I have a call on the other line." Once Precious has placed the call on hold, she starts talking to the phone, "You are a low-down dirty bum who thinks he's about to play with my feelings one more time." She clicks back over to Larry and says, "I've got to take this call."

Larry asks, "Are you going to call me back?"

Precious says with confidence, "No," and hangs up the phone.

Larry calls back. "What are you doing?"

"Larry, I don't want you anymore."

"You went down there and found someone else. Who is it?"

"The person I found is Precious Jennings, and she doesn't want you calling her anymore." Precious hangs up the phone and turns it off. She starts to leave the house when there is a knock at the door.

When she opens the door, there stand two White women.

Precious smiles. "Come on in."

"No, we can't. We just wanted to invite you to the neighborhood barbecue."

"Well, I was on my way out …"

"Just a few minutes, please?"

"Okay. I'll come over for only a few minutes."

They smile and lead Precious by the arm to the party.

"My name is Kathy, and this is Tammy."

"Nice to meet you. My name is Precious."

Precious can hear the laughter as she gets closer to the crowd of people. There are stacks of hamburgers, chips, and beer. Precious circles the lawn, meeting people. She looks into a man's face that is familiar to her; she can't remember where she saw him before. She finds there are several attorneys and doctors in the group. She learns that some of them are only at the cottage on the weekend and some have high-power jobs in Jacksonville and Columbus.

Several men have been drinking heavily and one says to her, "You know, you are the first Colored person to live in the cottages."

Precious is feeling very uncomfortable around these people and turns to leave, but turns around to confront the drinking man. "So, how do you know that there haven't been any Black people in the cottages?"

He staggers over to where she is standing. "It's common knowledge that there have been no Colored people living here."

"Well, there's a first time for everything. I'm glad I'm the first."

The man who looks familiar comes over to join the conversation. He asks Precious, "Aren't you getting ready to leave?"

Precious tells him, "Yeah. I'm out."

She is about to leave again when someone from the back of the crowds says, "Well, for sure you'll be the last."

Precious tells the group, "Well, if I'm going to be the last, I might as well stay and enjoy residence here. Oh, yeah, whoever sent me the note is a coward. How come you all don't leave this little place here, these cottages? All you do is sit around and mingle with the same people and circulate the same ideas." She is standing there waiting for someone to speak up and say something, anything, but no one says a word.

The man she thinks she knows from somewhere walks her out of the yard.

"Who are you?" Precious asks.

"Well, for right now, you can just call me your guardian angel. Now get out of here."

All the participants watch as Precious leaves. She is angry and kicks the grass beneath her feet.

Both Tammy and Kathy run after her.

Kathy says, "Please don't let that bother you. We're going to be here tonight and would like to invite you back. There's going to be a dance."

Precious doesn't want to come back. "My friend is in the hospital, and I plan to spend as much time with him as I can."

Tammy is saddened. "I'm sorry about your friend. We could have dinner waiting here for you when you come home tonight. If you don't feel like dancing with us, you can go home." Tammy puts her arm around Precious and says, "Deal?"

Precious smiles reluctantly and says, "Deal."

When Precious arrives at the McBride home she asks how Michael is.

Bertha, who has been weeping, says, "He's going to be all right. The bandages will come off in a week."

Precious breathes a sigh of relief.

"I guess you know by now Mrs. McBride isn't going to Washington."

"Yes, I figured she wouldn't go. Is anyone out looking for the people who did this to him?"

"I doubt it. I'll get Mrs. McBride for you."

The phone rings. Bertha turns back and asks Precious to answer it.

"Hello. This is the McBride residence."

"Who are you?"

"I'm Precious. Who would you like to speak to?"

"I want to speak to my husband, Michael."

"Could you hold on a minute, please?"

"You bet I'll hold on."

Mrs. McBride comes into the room, and Precious says, "This is Michael's ex-wife."

"I'll take it." Then she says, "Hello, dear."

"Hello. Can I talk to my husband?"

"He isn't here right now, and I don't expect him back for another week."

"Where is he?"

"He's indisposed at the time."

"What does that mean?"

"He can't come to the phone."

"Well tell him that I called."

"I'll do that, Rosa. Good-bye."

Mrs. McBride hangs up the phone.

Precious asks, "How come you didn't tell her where he is?"

"Young lady, she is not invited in my house. If Michael wasn't going to be well, I would have told her about the whole incident, but as much as possible, I'd like for her to live in her own house in California. I'm on my way to the hospital. Would you like to go?"

"Yes, I would."

"Let's go."

They ride most of the way without talking. Finally Mrs. McBride asks, "How long are you going to be with the agency?"

This question shocks Precious. It is something she has not thought about. Her answer shocks Mrs. McBride. "I don't know."

"Can you assure me that you'll be there for the life of this contract I'm about to sign? If you can't, I won't sign."

"I can't make that assurance. I wish I could, but I can't."

"Well then, I'm unsure about signing. I have a meeting downtown at four o'clock, and I must ask you to ride home with Wendy. She's at the hospital, and she can take you to my house to pick up your car."

On the way to the cottage from the hospital, Wendy promises Precious that she'll pick her up the next day and bring her to her car at Mrs. McBride's home. Precious is tired and doesn't feel like driving and is glad that Wendy is willing to take her home. After Wendy drops Precious off at the cottage, Precious starts to walk into her cottage when Tammy and Kathy approach her. "We saved food for you. Do you want it?"

Precious remembers that she hasn't eaten since lunch. "I would love the food. Where is it?"

Tammy says, "We left it at the grill. Come on over. You can get what you want, and you can go on home if you want to."

"I'm so tired. Yes, I would like to just get some food and go. I don't mean to be rude, but I need some sleep."

Kathy holds Precious by her arm. "Don't be silly. I know how that goes." The three women walk toward the party. When Precious looks at the faces in the group, she wonders if she is at a Halloween party in April. Everyone is dressed in black and white, and there is a zombie-like look on everyone's face. Their faces are painted in black and white.

"What is this?" Precious asks, wanting to leave right away, but both Tammy and Kathy have a firm grip on her arms.

"We're just having a little fun here. Come on in and join us."

Precious jerks away. "Sorry. I'm not into this kinda thing. I'll prepare my own food." Precious starts to leave but is grabbed from behind by someone who is much stronger than she is.

"Let me go," Precious says, trying to fight her way out of the grip.

"Come on, little lady. We're about to have a little fun with you." It is a man's voice, and no matter how hard Precious tries to fight, she is unable to get free.

Tammy smiles and says to Precious, "We're having a dance. It's called the Dance of Death. We're going to have a sacrifice this evening. We want the gods to bless us with long life, smart children, and wealth."

"Who are you going to sacrifice here tonight?" Precious is still fighting to be free.

Kathy says, "Don't you know by now? You're the sacrifice, sweetie. We all thought of you right away. Why, you're pretty, smart, and rich. We think the gods will be pleased with you. I know I am."

Precious cries out for help when someone else in the group puts his hand over her mouth. "Let's tie her up. Gag her, someone."

The group of zombie-like people dance wildly around the grill in the backyard as they chant "Death to you" over and over.

Finally the crowd gathers around Precious, who is now tied to a chair. They start to dance wildly around her, almost in a hypnotic-like trance.

"This happened too quick. How are we going to sacrifice her?" the leader asks the others.

"Let's have sex with her and then roast her like this pig."

"No, no," someone else says, "let's have sex with her and then hang her."

"No, no," another voice can be heard over the others, "I would rather burn her to death."

The group begins to argue and starts to push one another.

The familiar man from earlier in the day unties her and whispers, "You better run as fast as you can."

Precious takes off down the dirt road. She is almost a half a mile away before anyone notices that she is gone. They all start running after her. Precious can't even feel her heart beating. Her legs are long and she is taking gigantic steps as she sprints down the road toward the McBride estate. She continues to run, not feeling her feet beneath her.

The mansion is still a long ways away. She remembers the store and runs as fast as she can to it. The door is locked and the lights are off. She can see a car coming down the deserted road and she takes off running again as her life flashes before her. No matter how fast she runs, the car continues toward her faster. Finally she gives up and stops, knowing that her death is close by. She looks into the car, and it is the man who untied her.

"Hurry up and get into the car."

Without thinking, Precious gets in. "Who are you?" Precious says as she slumps over in the car.

"Ryan sent me. He paid me to come down to take care of you. He told me how your mother raised him and his siblings when his mother died. He told me how she would come up to the school and check on him all the time. He said that she's the reason he decided to go into the police department. It's strange. You never know how your helping someone else is going to come back to you. "

Precious doesn't say anything for several minutes as she digests what this man has just said to her. She finally says, "Did you follow me down here from Atlanta?"

"No. I got here when you moved in the cottage."

"Were you around my cottage early in the mornings?"

"Yes. I was trying to protect you."

"I love my cousin Ryan as if he were my brother."

"Yep, he loves you too. Do you know he told me that you wouldn't have sense enough to stay out of trouble? I didn't believe him." The man starts laughing. "Your cousin is going to have a fit when I tell him what happened to you. By the way, my name is Kevin. Since I've been here, I have gained another mission. It seems as though some people have been kidnapped, and they might be in this area."

Precious looks into the rearview mirror, and she can see people stopped in the road. It looks as though they are turning around and going back to their cottages.

"Well, I should be mad at Ryan, but this is one time I'm glad he had someone tailing me. Please take me over there." She motions toward the McBride estate. The car speeds down the road and within minutes Precious is at the McBride mansion, knocking on the door.

Kevin sits in the car until someone answers the door. "I'm with the Shalom Police Department," he says to Precious, "and I get my instructions from Ryan. I'll let you know in a couple of days how long I'll be here."

Precious is barely able to say "thanks" before the car speeds out of the driveway.

Bertha opens the door and finds Precious leaning against it. Bertha brings Precious into the house and leads her to a couch. She makes several phone calls and then goes into the kitchen to get water for Precious.

Bertha sits beside her. "I called the men in my family. They are on the Native-American reservation. They'll be here in a few minutes."

Chapter 17

April 25

Precious moves into the guesthouse on the McBride property. Because she is both embarrassed and ashamed of the way she has viewed the world, she doesn't leave her house for several days. She will not go up to the hospital to see about Michael because she is sure everyone is laughing at her. She does file a police report and tells the mayor what happened to her.

When Mrs. McBride finds out what happened to Precious and her quest for filing a police report, she knows that Precious is further humiliated about the incident because the police aren't doing anything about the occurrence.

Mrs. McBride brings food to the guesthouse. Precious expects to hear lectures from her, but Mrs. McBride only asks if Precious is all right. She holds Precious in her arms and rocks her ever so slowly, and Precious starts to cry.

"I should have listened to you. I'm sorry."

"Sorry? Precious, you shouldn't feel remorseful. You've learned a valuable lesson, one that no one could have taught you. I'm sure you'll be more careful today about the kind of people you allow into your personal space. I think that many of the problems you have are because you allowed the wrong people inside a most precious place."

Precious feels much better and accepted, now that Mrs. McBride has allowed her to move past the incident, and she talks openly and h o n e s tly with this woman about her feelings.

When Mrs. McBride gets up to leave, she hands Precious the contract. "I signed the contract. You don't have to stay here a minute longer. You're free to go home."

Precious inspects the contract, and even though she should feel happy, she doesn't.

"Mrs. McBride, do you think that signing this contract is going to get me to leave? I'm not running away from what they did to me. I'm staying here until I get some results." Precious then smiles and says, "If that's all right with you."

Mrs. McBride walks toward the door. "It's all right with me. But what are you fighting? The police and the mayor aren't going to help you with your situation. I would help you, but I have other problems I need to attend to. Now, if you can't help us with our cause, you might as well go on back to Michigan because with anything else you're wasting your time."

Precious goes to the police station again and talks with several men. The police tell her that they'll investigate the occurrence, but by their body language Precious can deduce they won't exert any energy on the case. She decides for now to drop her cause and help Mrs. McBride.

She is surprised with the amount of support she is receiving from people in the community. Dozens of men from the town go back to the cottage with shotguns in their hands to retrieve Precious's belongings.

Chapter 18

May 5

Michael is back home after hours of grueling therapy. He walks with a limp, and his face is badly bruised. He is unable to farm the land, so the family hires several men to work in his place. He hears about what happened to Precious and hobbles to the guesthouse to see her.

"How are you, Cowboy?"

"I've been better."

He sits down on the couch in front of the television. There is another late-breaking report about the kidnapped people. The police think that the people who were kidnapped are now dead.

Precious says, "I witnessed one of the kidnappings."

"Which one?"

"Jessica. I called my cousin in the police department back home, but it was too late. I will always live with that in my mind."

Michael touches his head. "I'll always live with the fact that I got beat up. I've never gotten beat up before…. It was just too many of them. I know it was the same group of people who ran you out of the cottage who beat me up. I think I would have been dead if I hadn't run."

Precious is astonished. "I ran too. I remember how this woman told me how I ran pretty. I was insulted until I really had to run for my life. I don't feel insulted anymore. As a matter of fact, it feels rather good.

I've crossed over to the other side of life now. All the cute running was out the window as I ran for my life. I didn't care how I looked. I didn't care what I was wearing or how my hair looked or even the amount of sweat on my face. If I had stopped I know I would have been killed. I've never been that close to death."

Michael sits back, more relaxed. "Me either. So how are we going to console each other?"

Precious has an idea. "Well, I've got some chicken in the refrigerator. Bertha brought it out to me and she demanded that I eat it for my health. We could grill."

"That's not what I had in mind, but it'll do for now."

Michael tries to help her with the grill and finally gives up and goes over and searches the music collection she brought with her. He is elated when he finds something he likes, Wayman Tisdale with an old Smoky Robinson song, "Cruisin'." Michael says, "I would dance with you, but I can't right now."

Precious smiles. "For now, you heal from your physical ailments, and I'm going to try to heal from my psychological trauma. One day, we shall dance together."

Chapter 19

May 10

Michael is a little grouchy as he descends the stairs. Mrs. McBride has been gone all day, and no one seems to know where she is.

Wendy is in the living room.

"Hello, big brother."

Michael limps to a seat near the fireplace. He says to his sister, "What are you up to?"

"You do remember that some friends and I are developing an all-natural makeup kit, and we were wondering if you could help us out some. There is a component missing, and we think the colors are wrong, and since you aren't working now, I was wondering if you could take a look."

"I would love to. Maybe tomorrow morning."

"Thanks. Do you want me to bring you something to eat, big brother?"

"No, I'm not hungry. Where's Mom?"

"I don't know. I thought you knew. She always tells someone when she's going to be gone a long period of time. Maybe she told Bertha."

Bertha is on her way upstairs when she hears her name and joins them in the living room.

"What are you talking about?"

Michael tries to turn in the direction where Bertha is standing. "Where did Mom go?"

"I don't know where she could be now. She went to a meeting in town this morning.

Michael then asks, "How long has she been gone?"

Bertha looks up at the grandfather clock in the corner of the room. "She's been gone since ten this morning."

"Where did she say she was going?"

Bertha feels as though she is being interrogated as she says again, "She told me that she was going to a meeting in town and that she would be back around one."

Wendy says, "It's almost four. She should be coming home soon."

Michael makes several attempts to get off the couch and on the third try he is successful. "I'll call her cell phone."

The phone just keeps ringing, then goes to voice mail. Michael decides to hang up. He thinks for several seconds. He remembers the news report of kidnappings and his discussion about the kidnappings with Precious. He thinks about the recent incidents with Precious and with him and he is alarmed. He finally says, "I don't like it. Is she with Precious?"

Both Wendy and Bertha hunch their shoulders, indicating they have no idea where Mrs. McBride could be.

The phone rings and Michael picks it up. "Hello."

"Hello, Michael. This is Mr. Lane. How are you doing?"

"I'm making progress every day."

"Good. Good for you. Um, your mother's car has been in my parking lot all day. Is she at home?"

"No. No, she isn't."

"Is it possible that she could be with your young lady friend?"

"I don't know. I'll give her a call."

"Good. I'll check around town and see if I see her. Call me back on my cell phone if she turns up."

"I will."

Precious is standing on the porch at Mrs. McBride's guesthouse. She has just finished talking to Dwight DeVeux, who at times was pleading and at other times demanding that Precious return to her job. Finally she tells him that she will take a vacation for several weeks.

He has called her every day since Mrs. McBride signed the contract. De Veux is reluctant to give her the time off until she reminds him that she is his partner. Now, standing on the porch, she feels powerful and is debating whether to go jogging around the countryside on Mrs. McBride's property when the phone rings.

"Precious, this is Michael. Is my mother back there?"

"No. I saw her earlier today at your home. I haven't seen her since then."

"She drove into town today. They found her car in Dan Lane's store parking lot. Nobody has seen her."

Precious can tell his voice is shaking and she becomes concerned too.

Michael says, "I thought maybe she came back there."

"Where are you?" Precious asks. She stands at attention as though she might be going into battle.

"I'm at the house. I'm about to go out and look for her."

"I'll be there in a minute." Precious hangs up the phone and starts looking for her keys. She has a key holder in the kitchen and usually this is where she can find them. She searches frantically, turning over cushions and pillows in the living room. Since the incident with the Knights of Darkness, she always locks all her doors. Several minutes pass before she finds the keys on the nightstand in her bedroom. She is out of the guesthouse and running toward the mansion in minutes.

Michael meets Precious at the door. "The police have been called and they are out looking for her." He takes Precious's hand and leads her through the door. Everyone in Mrs. McBride's family is there, worried.

Precious notices that Wendy and Bertha are staring at Michael and at her.

"Hello," Precious says as she sees the anxious looks on their faces. "We'll find her."

Michael, who is watching her, states, "All I know is that she had a meeting downtown with the Black farmers. I called them when I got off the phone with you, and they said that they had an eleven o'clock meeting and that she didn't show up. There is no trace of her. I'm scared. My mother is diabetic and has to take insulin."

"Well, did you ask them why they didn't call the house once she hadn't showed up for the meeting?"

Michael walks closer to Precious and says, "Yeah, I did. If she says she's going to a meeting, she always goes. They told me that they called the house and her cell phone and didn't get an answer."

Bertha thinks quickly. "That had to be right around the time I went down to the corner store. I got a call saying that my check had bounced. I knew better than that. They asked me to come take care of it right away. I wasn't thinking, I didn't turn the answering machine on because I knew it was only going to take a minute to straighten things out. When I got there, the owner told me he hadn't called me. Odd." Bertha stands there thinking about the situation.

Precious can see the worried expression on Bertha's and Michael's faces. She feels so helpless—there is not much she can do. "I'm going to make a pot of coffee." Precious whisks out of the room. As she turns the coffee maker on, she thinks, *She'll turn up, and I won't cry. She'll be home soon. I just can't lose another important person in my life.*

As she composes her body and mind, she brings cups into the living room. People start arriving, all asking the same questions.

Precious whispers to Michael, "I don't see Mr. Lane." Michael points into the middle of the room, and there stands Dan Lane. He appears to be giving instructions to someone he is talking to.

There are men in business suits and little old ladies and old men. A group of men in overalls with guns are standing up against the wall.

"This doesn't make sense. If all the people she knows are in this room, where could she be?" Precious expects an answer from Michael.

Michael shakes his head. "I don't know." Precious's mind goes back to the day she saw Jessica kidnapped and for several seconds she has cold chills.

Hours pass, and there is no sign of Mrs. McBride. The men in the overalls decide that the police are taking too long in their search, and they decide to mount their own search for Mrs. McBride. The others stay and are waiting patiently for a visit or a call from the police. The police assured the family earlier in the day that everything would turn out all right, yet they haven't called or been back to the mansion with any news. This has angered Michael, but he is managing to keep calm.

He says to the thirty-five guests who are still there, "Is anyone hungry?"

No one says a word, and for the first time, Michael doesn't know what to do.

Finally at four in the morning, Michael says to several men who are still awake, "I'm going down to the police station."

"Why don't you call them?" Mr. Lane steps forward, looking more in control than Michael.

"I want to see just what they're doing down there."

Precious says, "I'll drive."

"No, you won't drive. This town isn't safe right now. I'm not going to have people chasing you around. I want you to stay here. I don't want to have to worry about anyone but my mother right now. Mr. Lane and Rickey, will y'all go down there with me?"

They nod, then leave together like soldiers reporting for combat.

When Michael walks into the Star police station, there are only three police officers in the entire building. He approaches an officer he knows, one he has known all his life. They played together as children, but for some strange reason Robert's family decided that he needed to find other friends.

"Robert, did you find my mother?"

Robert slowly shakes his head. There is a worried expression on his face too. "We've had men out all night looking for her. We even have police in other counties watching out for her. We haven't heard anything, and that's unusual."

Robert looks carefully at Michael and Mr. Lane and Ricky and decides that he will tell them the truth. "We have had, in the past three months, four outspoken people disappear from neighboring towns. Two of them showed up and the other two we're still looking for."

There, the truth was out. Robert wonders, *How are they going to handle the truth?*

Michael walks right up to Robert and gets close to his face. "You mean to tell me that this has happened before and you haven't told anyone?"

"No, because they weren't in this county. I didn't think we had anything to worry about."

Mr. Lane steps between Michael and Robert, saying, "Are you still looking for the two people who are missing?"

"No. But the other county is still looking."

"Where are they looking tonight?" Mr. Lane asks, being the only one in control in the room.

"Well, the sheriff went out looking. I think he went to several bars."

Mr. Lane is flabbergasted. "Bars? Mrs. McBride would not be going to bars."

Robert scratches his head. "I told the sheriff she wouldn't be in a bar. He told me I was crazy and that he knew that, but maybe someone in the bar knows where she is."

Michael moves in face to face with Robert. "Tell the sheriff that I'll be back later today to find out what he knows."

Mr. Lane takes a deep breath and says, "Has anyone gone to Mrs. McBride's car?"

Robert is proud to say yes, he has been there.

Mr. Lane says, "Did you find anything unusual?"

"Well, no, we didn't."

Mr. Lane plants both hands on Robert's desk and says, "Her car was unlocked. She never leaves her car unlocked."

Robert explains that this is no big deal.

Mr. Lane is getting angrier as he says, "Did you notice anything else?"

Robert doesn't like the questioning and roughly says, "No."

Mr. Lane yells, "Her hat was in the car. She never goes anywhere without a hat."

Chapter 20

Mrs. McBride is positioned between two large men. Even though there is a mask over her face preventing her from seeing, she can tell by the voices that they are strong men. She tries to act tough, but her quivering lips do not mask her true feelings. "Why me?" Her voice is barely audible and the men talking keep their flow of conversation going.

"I don't know," she hears as one man tries to answer the other man's inquiry.

"I think we're supposed to take the car to the drop-off point."

Mrs. McBride hears one man say to the driver, "Turn to the right and go down there a couple of blocks."

Once again Mrs. McBride finds enough words and courage to say, "I want to know where you are taking me."

"Shut up and just ride and you might live long enough to see tomorrow."

"Do you know who I am?" Mrs. McBride sits up straight to show that she carries some weight in the community.

Both men sitting with her start to laugh. As they think about her between the two of them, they begin to laugh even harder.

Once they have settled down, one man says, "Yes, we know who you are. Why do you think you're sitting here with your hands bound and eyes blindfolded?"

Mrs. McBride finally begins to realize the seriousness of her predicament. "I will have all of you locked up in jail."

Mrs. McBride can hear and sense the back window going down and a cool breeze coming through the window. A man finally says, "You better hope that you'll see tomorrow."

"Why are you kidnapping me?" Mrs. McBride pleads with them. "Do you want my money? I'll give you all of it. Please, just let me out of here."

"Relax, lady. We don't want your money. I'll tell you why you're here, though. It's because you're the leader of that movement. If you weren't the leader, you wouldn't be here right now, so shut up. When you decided to lead, you must of thought that as a leader, you might die. Don't ask us anything else."

Mrs. McBride is quiet for the rest of the two-hour bumpy ride, but her mind is racing as she contemplates her own death. She thinks, *Did I treat other people right? Is my will up to date? How will I be remembered? Will my children come to look for me? Will I ever see them again?*

Finally, the car stops and there are several minutes of silence, although Mrs. McBride can tell that they are communicating in a way she doesn't understand.

"Get out," she is told by one of the men in the backseat.

Her hands are bound behind her back. "I'm not a criminal. I don't know where you're taking me, and I'm not getting out of this car."

"Yes, you are."

Mrs. McBride is pushed out of the car. She lands on the ground and tastes the dirt beneath her head. She is sure that she is hurt but can't feel any part of her body. She lies there wondering why.

Several seconds later, Mrs. McBride is pulled to her feet.

"Get down those stairs."

"What stairs?"

"Come on. I'll lead you." Mrs. McBride is careful as she places one foot in front of the other. She is close to falling again and would like to just crawl to her destination—at least she will be able to feel her way around. The only thing she knows that she can count on are her instincts, and they tell her that she might be all right for a little while. She walks several feet before being shoved. A door locks behind her. She can sense that there are other people in the room with her.

"Hello … um … I need help. Can anybody help me?"

A voice from across the room says, "Ah, look, we're going to share our lovely accommodations with another person." The voice sounds flat and impoverished.

"I beg your pardon? As you can see, I have something over my eyes preventing me from seeing. Would you please untie me so that I might become familiar with my surroundings?"

Footsteps walk closer to her. "She's an old lady."

"I know how old I am, and I have life in my years." Mrs. McBride is forgetting how frightened she is and replaces those emotions with anger. "Untie me, you quivering excuse for a human being. Untie me now."

The blindfold drops from her eyes, and for several seconds she tries to focus on her new surroundings. While her vision is clearing, she feels someone behind her untying her hands. She gazes around, staring at five conquered people sprawled around the room, staring at the new arrival.

Mrs. McBride glances at the new plaster on the walls and checks out the room, avoiding the eyes staring at her. There are no windows. There is only one small room in the corner with a toilet and a small shower.

She thinks, *Thank God there is a door to the bathroom.* The tiny sink in the small room is large enough to wash hands. The smell of their bodies tells Mrs. McBride that they have been confined for more than four days.

Mrs. McBride then focuses on the five people in the room with her.

"Who has the audacity to talk to me as if I am deficient?" she hears herself saying with fire in her eyes.

"I did." A White man stands up and drops his head in embarrassment. He then sits back down, seemingly holding up the wall behind him. Mrs. McBride sums him up in her thoughts. *He appears to be someone who talks quite candidly and probably is even more derogatory about people when he's in the comfort of his own home.*

Mrs. McBride stares angrily at him for almost fifteen seconds as she examines him. "That's the trouble with people who think they're better than other people. You and I are in the same predicament, and you have the nerve to act as though you somehow have the right to think you're better than anyone else. For someone who's in the same quandary as everybody else, I would say that you're a foolish man."

"Yeah, he is a fool, lady. You got that right." A White woman from the corner of the room stands up and walks over. "He's been here the longest and hasn't found a way out of here."

An Arab man walks over to the group. "Hello, my man is Abu Malik Aziz bin Baaz, which means that I am from the family of Baaz. I came to this country to attend school at Princeton. I am from Syria. I am a long ways from home. My family calls me the bright one. Before I was kidnapped, I was a well-respected economist employed by the United Nations."

Mrs. McBride walks over to him, not believing the situation she finds herself in. "If you are so well respected, how come people aren't out looking for you?"

Abu shrugs in disbelief. "Well, I believe they're looking for me, but they know that I have strange ways. My family knows that I often go away alone. I have bad news to present to the United Nations. I had to get away to think about my findings and decide whether I am going to share this news with others."

Before Abu is able to say more, a young Native-American man stands to his feet. "I am Nantan Yuma Smith. Nantan means 'spokesman' in Apache. I graduated at the top of my class at Northwestern University. My degree is in environmental studies. I am employed at Rossman Research Center. The company gets its money from the federal government. My job is spending time among the lakes, rivers, and forests, bringing back water and soil samples to the laboratory for research and comparative studies. I, too, have bad news to report."

DeShan Williams, who appears to be the youngest in the group, stands to his feet as though it is his turn to introduce himself. His thick dreadlocks hang down his back, and everyone can tell that his locks are his pride and joy as he swings them back and forth as he walks.

"My name is DeShan Williams, and I'm a rapper. I rap about everything, from ghetto life to dropping discarded missiles from World War II in the lakes and oceans. I was about to release my next single when I was kidnapped at the airport in Los Angeles and brought here on a private plane. What the hell is going on here?"

The middle-aged White woman who is standing next to Mrs. McBride rubs her hand across her dress. She is a little nervous as she says to Mrs. McBride, "Well, my name is Jessica Zellman. I guess you can call me a troublemaker. I ran for state senator in Michigan two times and was defeated two times. I am just a middle-class mother of two adult children who is sick and tired of other countries dumping their trash in Michigan. There's a dump site close to where I live.

Everyone says that these sites are doing no harm. I disagree. I believe that they are. I wasn't going to take a stand until one evening I was driving home and saw what I thought was the largest rat I had ever seen. But it was much bigger than a rat. I was brought up in the country and, quite frankly, I don't know what that creature was. For the first time in my life, I was frightened, startled because I have no idea what it was and how many are out there growing in those dump sites. I had just finished writing to the local newspaper and my article appeared the day before I was kidnapped."

The White man who had been quiet since Mrs. McBride's words with him says he realizes that his destiny is tied to everyone else who is in the room. "My name is Richard Wyle. I've been sitting in the corner since my first day here trying to figure out what we all have in common. I raise organic cattle in Nebraska. My mission in life is to give the American people the best food supply. That way, we can keep our citizens healthy and better able to make good decisions about their destiny. Two months ago, I got into trouble with the other ranchers in my area because I exposed mad cow disease. I went to the local government and was turned away. I wrote to the Agriculture Department and asked them to come out and investigate my charges. They never came out, but some of my neighbors did. I was told that if I wrote another letter that all my cattle would somehow come down with the same disease."

Mrs. McBride finally says, "I am the spokesman for the local Black farmers. We haven't been able to find fair trade for our food. Because of that, many farmers are going bankrupt. We've approached the government for help financially, and not much has happened. I've been trading with other countries. Even though I don't have a problem trading with other countries, I believe that I have a right to choose where I'll take my goods."

Mrs. McBride studies the expression of each member of the group.

Everyone is scared. Even though she doesn't know them, their fear is one thing she knows for sure.

She finally says, "I'm trying to figure out what we all have in common too. Richard, who is a cattle farmer, appears to be the only person I have something in common with. Abu and Nantan were about to deliver bad news, Jessica wrote a letter to a newspaper, and DeShan … from what I see so far, DeShan seems to be an outspoken person. I'm wondering if someone in society sees us as a threat to a way of life."

Chapter 21

Precious sits pensively, staring directly at the beige phone in the guesthouse, a position she's maintained for the last half hour. The pain of losing both parents and now a surrogate mother leaves her feeling powerless. She searches her mind for someone to call, someone who will understand her pain. Finally, absently, she starts dialing a familiar number. The phone rings twice before Precious hears someone pick up the phone.

"Hello," comes a seductive voice on the other end of the phone.

"Hi, Sis. How are you?"

"Precious, are you all right? I was in the newsroom late last night, and I heard about that lady being kidnapped in Star. I tried to get you all last night. Was your phone turned off?"

"No. I left the phone at the guesthouse. I spent the night at Mrs. McBride's house."

"I thought you were living in a cottage."

"That's a long story, and we can talk about that later."

"I'm glad you're all right. I was just about to come down there. Look, are you coming home or do you want me there?"

"Jazzy, I need you down here. The police aren't telling us anything, and frankly, I don't think they know anything. I want you to bring your investigating skills down here plus any contacts you might have. I really need you, Sis. Tell Ryan that you're coming and find out what he knows about the disappearance of Mrs. McBride. Also tell him that I met his friend, Kevin, the one he sent down here to watch over me."

"What? Ryan sent someone down there?"

"Yep. I'm really glad he did. I want you to meet him when you get here. Find out from Ryan where Kevin is staying."

"I'll make reservations today. I'll talk to people at the television station today about contacts. I'll stop by Ryan's home tonight. Don't worry. You and I together will see this thing through. I'm doing this for you, Precious.

"Thanks, Jazzy. Let me know what time your plane gets in."

"I will."

Precious hangs up the phone more confident as she creeps around the room searching for her purse. Once she finds it, she is out the door and heads toward the McBride mansion.

As Precious starts to ring the doorbell, Wendy opens the door. She's dressed in all black with a veil over her face. "Come in" is all she can manage to say.

"Have you heard anything yet? What's happened?"

Wendy shakes her head, and for the first time Precious notices how vulnerable Wendy is. Precious has seen the same look on her own face for the last three months and immediately gives Wendy a needed hug. She decides to hug Wendy like Mrs. McBride hugged her. Wendy doesn't resist. She has wanted and needed someone who would just touch her.

"I can't imagine what you're going through right now, but I want you to know that I'm not going anywhere until this thing is finished."

"Thanks, Precious. To be honest with you, I knew you were all right all the time. I just wanted to give you a hard time. I know we're going to find her."

Finally Precious asks again, "Have you heard anything yet?"

"No. The police can't seem to find any leads in this case. They've called in the FBI. They should be in town later today."

When they finally back away from each other, sensing that the closeness is too much for either one of them to take at the moment, Precious asks, "Where is Cow— Michael?"

"He went to the airport."

"Who is he picking up?"

"His ex-wife."

"What … what is she doing here?"

"Michael and Rosa broke up in the first place because Daddy was real sick. Michael asked her to come help take care of Daddy, the mansion, Mama, and the farm. She said, 'Shiiitttttt,' she had a good job, and she wasn't leaving. When Daddy died, do you know she didn't even come to the funeral. Now he's at the Jackson airport picking that heifa up. Life sure is funny."

Precious sits there for several minutes trying to decide if she wants to be there when the two arrive. She decides that she would much rather go to the police station to see for herself if they've found out anything.

"I'll see you later. I'm going into town."

"Can I go with you?"

The expression on Wendy's face says that she needs to retreat from the situation. Precious can see that this is the beginning of the bonding process with this young woman, and she isn't sure that she wants to bond with Wendy because of Wendy's weird personality. It takes several seconds before Precious makes up her mind. "Yeah, come on. Let's go."

The police assure Precious and Wendy that they are doing all they can to find Mrs. McBride. Sergeant Wilbert Brock promises that he'll come out to the mansion or call if he has any information.

Precious and Wendy walk over to Mr. Lane's grocery store. Mr. Lane is standing behind the counter of the information desk when the two women walk inside.

"Hello, ladies. Have you heard anything yet?"

Wendy, who is still draped in a black veil, approaches the counter first. "No, we haven't heard a word. Have you heard anything?"

Mr. Lane rubs the back of his head. Immediately the two women know he has heard something, but he isn't sure if he wants to tell them.

"Yeah. I got a call from some people I met in Washington. I was told that there have been several kidnappings in the past week, and they think they're all related in some way. Somethin' ain't right."

Mr. Lane walks over to the ice cream. "You want some ice cream on the house?"

After thanking Mr. Lane for the ice cream, the two are out the door into the steaming hot weather.

"Come on. Let's take a walk," Precious says, remembering the walk that she and Mrs. McBride took several weeks ago. They sit under a tree while looking out over the meadow. For a long time, neither one says a word, waiting to hear what the other has to say. Finally Precious says, "As soon as we find your mother, I'll be going home."

"Are you going home because Rosa is here?"

"No. I was planning on going home when Mrs. McBride signed the contract, and then this happened. I'm not going to leave here until there's some closure. I don't care how long it takes. There's nothing between Cowboy and me, just another person I met."

Wendy says, directing her thoughts into the air, "Michael has been out organizing search parties, questioning people who were in and out of Mr. Lane's store, searching through names of visitors at the local hotel, and pestering the police department, which seems to be ignoring this case, and he still hasn't come up with anything.

"I can tell you, Precious, this is bad timing that his ex-wife decides to come now. Michael's doctors have told him to take it easy, that he can reopen his wounds if he isn't careful. Now Rosa is here. I can't stand her."

They sit for thirty more minutes. Even though the sweat rolls down their faces like water, they still sit and take pleasure in each other's silence. Wendy thinks, *This is the first best friend I have ever had besides my mother.* She has much more respect for Precious. She respects Precious for staying in town and helping in the search for her mother and for taking time to talk to her as if she's an adult.

Finally, the inevitable moment comes. "Come on, Wendy. I'm going to take you home."

They drive down the dusty road, not saying anything to each other. When they drive up to the mansion, Michael's truck is outside. "Are you coming in?"

"Yeah, I wanna come in." Precious is out of the car in a flash as she follows Wendy into the house.

There, sitting in the living room, is the most sophisticated woman Precious has ever seen and she has seen plenty. Even though the temperature has reached over 105 degrees, this woman is sitting in the living room drinking hot coffee with a white short-sleeve suit on. Her stiletto white heels match the white in the dress perfectly. Her hair is in an upward sweep with curls falling to both sides of her head and in the back. Her makeup is impeccable, and her flawless confidence matches the way she is dressed, perfect.

Precious stands there dripping in sweat. Her hair has wilted under the sun. Several ice-cream stains are on her short-sleeve washable dress. There is dirt on the back of her dress from sitting on the hill. Her shoes are dusty and muddy. Her makeup melted under the rays of the sun several hours ago.

But with all the negatives affecting Precious at this moment, her confidence level is high, even higher than usual. She seems to have gotten to the point in life where she has finally realized that inner beauty takes precedence over outward show.

"Hello. My name is Precious. How was your flight?" Precious extends her hand, but Rosa backs away, concerned that she might somehow catch the vibrations coming from Precious's unkempt appearance.

"It was a most lovely flight. A little turbulence, but I was able to make it through it."

"Damn, girl," Wendy blurts out, "you ain't changed a bit. I see you are still stuck on yourself."

"Ahh, Wendy. I didn't recognize you under that black lace veil. Still a weird, confused child, I see."

Precious thinks to herself, *If it wasn't for the fact that Mrs. McBride is missing, I could have a field day with this woman talking to Wendy like that when she has to know how upset Wendy must be.*

"I'm sorry, what is your name?" Precious says, not giving away that Wendy has already told her about Rosa. "You seem to be taking advantage of a young woman who has just had her mother kidnapped."

Rosa glares into Precious's eyes, realizing that she is going to have to bring out her armor with this woman. "My name is Rosa McBride, and I don't need anyone to tell me how to talk to Wendy. You see, we go way back, much further than you and her, and a lot longer than you and Michael."

"Your name ain't McBride no more," Wendy says, circling Rosa as though she is trying to intimidate an opponent. "And even though you go back much further than Precious, I can tell you that this family likes her a lot more than we like you."

Rosa, sensing that she is standing alone, replies, "I never dropped that name 'cause I knew that I would be picking it up again. I have history with Michael, and I know where his pleasure sensors are."

Wendy is laughing as she says, "We ain't trying to reach Michael's pleasure sensors. Please, you silly woman, we're trying to find my mother, and if you aren't down for that, take your Miss Manners ass back to California 'cause we were doing just fine without you."

Michael is standing in the doorway listening to the verbal exchange. Precious is standing there ready to back Wendy up. Precious's hair is falling in her face. Michael is amused and Precious can tell he is as she says, "I'm glad you have some support, Michael. I can see why you didn't like me when we first met."

Precious catches her words and stops and refocuses her attention on the present situation. "My sister will be here tomorrow. We have enough people here to find Mrs. McBride, and I know we'll find her."

Michael stands next to Precious as if he is about to kiss her for the first time, but remembers there are other people in the room. "I'm glad your sister is coming. I want you and her to come over for dinner tomorrow night. I would like to prepare dinner for you."

At this, Rosa clears her throat, and Michael says, "And you, too, Rosa."

Rosa gives Precious a fierce stare before saying, "Michael, you won't have time to cook dinner for her. Your mother is missing, and you and I will find her … together. We don't need all these people down here anyway."

"I'm cooking dinner for Precious and her sister. Now if you don't want to be here, that's on you."

"Well, I guess I'll be going," Precious says. "If you hear anything, would you please let me know?"

"Wait, I'll walk you out to your car." Michael dashes across the room.

As they walk out the door, Precious tells him about the trip to the police station and the conversation with Mr. Lane. Michael tells her that he will be meeting with the FBI later that night and will call her with any information. As he opens the car door for her, they stand and stare into each other's eyes for several seconds before breaking the spell.

"I'll see you later," Precious says as Michael closes the door. As she pulls out of the driveway, Michael is watching her as she drives toward the guesthouse, and for several seconds he thinks about following her.

Chapter 22

DeShan and Nantan walk quietly around the small room, searching for an escape. There is none. Their captors have thought of everything. Nantan concludes that the structure is magnificently made and their captors have an immense knowledge of building designs. Fresh air is flowing through the room, yet no one knows how it is flowing. The ceiling recedes a quarter of its length during the day, then closes at night. In the morning four gunmen who wear masks bring in food. Because of Mrs. McBride's diabetes, they bring medication and measuring devices for her.

Mrs. McBride pleads with them to bring her a hat that coordinates with her blue dress and, surprisingly, they do.

Abu, who seems almost relieved to be kidnapped, sits next to a wall leaning back as though he is on a deserted island in the Caribbean. He watches as DeShan and Nantan walk slowly around the room and as Mrs. McBride walks into the bathroom and closes the door. When she finally comes out, she says to no one in particular, "I wonder why they haven't killed us."

Nantan, who has thought about this, says, "Why did they bring the six of us together?"

Mrs. McBride, who has been recognized as the leader of the group, stands in front of them as though she is putting the pieces together as they all sit around her waiting for her to tell them some good news.

"Tell me this, Abu, what was the bad news you were going to report to the government?"

Abu, who has expected someone to ask him this question, is still not prepared to respond to the group.

"Well … uh … I completed research in regards to globalism." He gazes around the room and realizes that the other captives are smart enough to understand his findings, but decides to start off with a question. "Do you know what deliberate preobligation is?"

Jessica smiles and says, "Yeah, I know what it is. It's starting a diet that is the deliberate action, and preobligation is suffering the consequences if I eat too much."

Abu laughs. "Jessica, you're in the ballpark of the problem. A deliberate preobligation in simple terms means only that a person or persons have made a commitment to do something, and if they don't do their part, there are going to be consequences."

DeShan says, "You mean, Brother Abu, that if I go in to rob a corner grocery store and tell everyone in there that if they don't give me the money in the cash register, that I'm going to shoot everyone in there?"

Abu smiles. "That's exactly what I mean. The deliberate action is to rob the store, and the preobligation is that if those in the store don't do as you say, then you're going to shoot them. Without going into details, this is going on globally, that is, certain people are taking over the world, and I was going to bring this travesty to the attention of the United Nations, and I am kinda happy I was brought here."

DeShan says, "Everyone knows this is going on, man. What makes it so special coming from you?"

Abu ponders for a moment, then says, "I have evidence. I have names, and I have a specific date when there will be a takeover."

Richard enters the conversation with, "The United Nations isn't going to listen to what you have to say. They must hear this kind of thing all the time."

Abu turns to Richard and says, "Who do you think is in control of the United Nations?"

Richard smiles and says, "We all know who is running the United Nations. Whose soil is it on?"

Abu fixes his soiled tie and whispers to the whole group, "The United Nations has a branch of operation where all the subcommittees do is listen to scientists and world leaders. Their job is to take corrective action. The subcommittees are run by Kenya, Bulgaria, South Africa, India, Japan, and Sweden. Not a lot of people know this. These countries are really interested in what's going on, and they have the power to stop any takeover. There is so much money in these countries and this is why they control things."

Richard starts laughing. "Man, you are totally off your rocker, and these countries don't have money. They're always begging other countries to help them."

Abu says, "You may believe what you will, but what I say is true. I would rather be here with you than have to go speak the truth, but I know that once I leave here, I'm going to have to tell the truth—if I make it out of here."

The room is quiet as they scrutinize what Abu has just said. Jessica would like to ask more questions, but she has seen that Abu has shared more than he had planned to.

Richard turns to Nantan, who is sitting next to him. "What were you going to the government to tell them?"

Nantan is apprehensive but is ready to speak up now that Abu has spoken. "I've been studying carbon storage. In this study, I've examined the forest range. Did you know that the value of a forest is between $360 and $2,200 per hectare? If we continue to destroy the forest, we are going to lose it." He turns to Richard and says, "Even grazing for cattle can be destroying the world. You see, my research has found that it is more cost effective to conserve the forest than to clear them.

"In addition, I have asked for money to kill the *Pueraria lobata*, in other words the kudzu. This plant is killing the trees by choking them to death."

DeShan speaks up, "You mean those vines that wrap themselves around trees and homes?"

"Yep. They may look like nice little vines, but they're killing our trees. You have no idea what a vast wasteland this world will be without trees. God in his infinite wisdom made trees so that we can breathe. I'm trying to save our lives as well as the trees."

Mrs. McBride thinks for several minutes. No one says a word as they wait for her. "Richard, you are a cattle farmer. Is that correct?"

"Yes, you would be correct in saying that I'm a cattle farmer, but you would be even more on the mark if you counted me as one of the best cattle farmers in this country."

"So you love your profession, do you?"

"Yes. I love being out there in the open fields."

Mrs. McBride moves in closer to him. "What makes your business better than others?"

Richard is excited to discuss what he does. He looks around the room, and everyone is waiting to hear what he has to say. Even though they are trying to find the connection as to why they were all brought to this place, Richard is more interested in telling them what he does. No one has ever been interested before, not even his wife.

"I feed my cattle top grain, and every day I am out there cleaning up after the cattle. We are very humane in how we kill our cattle. I've seen the way the cattle ranches kill, and it is sickening. If any part of the animal is diseased, I won't send any part of the animal to market. This is not true for most ranches. Some will just cut out the diseased spot and send the rest of the carcass to market. I would never do that. There should be some dignity in the cattle industry."

DeShan cannot believe his ears. "So when I go into a restaurant and order a steak, what should I consider?"

Richard loves the question and smiles as he says, "You should consider what part of the animal the beef is coming from. The most tender beef comes from those muscles along the back and the midsection of the animal, only for one reason. That reason is this is the place where animals exercise the least."

Mrs. McBride is more interested in the politics of his business. She says, "How does the government grade your animals?"

Richard looks around the room, and everyone is still listening, "Well, the government consists of the United States as well as Canada, and they use a labeling system. I believe they have a pretty good guide in deciding marbling."

Abu asks, "What is marbling?"

Richard says, "Marbling refers to the flecks of fat within a cut of meat, especially in the lean muscle of the meat. I have stringent requirements with my cattle, and they've been making the grade. I think other cattle farmers are a little jealous because with them, only one in twelve makes the grade."

"Well," says Mrs. McBride, "we are all advocating for a better life in some form or another."

Abu examines every word Richard said, but doesn't say anything.

"I'm hungry," DeShan says. "I haven't had a nice cut of steak in months. I need to eat."

Everyone nods in agreement.

Minutes pass, and everyone waits for Mrs. McBride's next words. "DeShan, what is your stage name?"

No one had asked him that since he has been there. "My name is A-Knowledge."

Mrs. McBride asks, "What does the A stand for?"

"The A stands for Achieve. I'm always going to be achieving and using good judgment in the way that I rap. In the contract I just signed I was told that I would be making adverse statements about teenagers like myself. I told them I wouldn't do it. Unfortunately, I didn't read the fine print where it said I would be making the kind of music that they will produce and that they would have to give their seal of approval for all my raps. My attorney said he didn't catch it. But I think he did and they just paid him off. I was sold down the river."

Mrs. McBride asks, "Well then, what are you going to do about it?"

"First, I'm going to write the kind of music I can be proud of. Then I'm going to hire an ethical attorney and we're going to fight. When I'm told to make other kinds of rap, I'll hold true to what I believe."

Jessica says, "You'll give in. People always give in when money is involved."

DeShan says, "We'll see, won't we."

Mrs. McBride nods. "Yes, we'll see what you are made of. Would you please rap for us?"

Jessica covers her ears and loudly says, "No, I don't want to hear any rap."

Mrs. McBride turns to Jessica. "What is your problem?"

She says, without thinking, "It's ghetto music. They're always talking about bitches and whores. They want to shoot somebody and kill the police, and they have no regard for their mothers."

DeShan, who is about to defend his music, is waved down by Mrs.

McBride. "Well, young lady, you have just created another stereotype. All rap music isn't about hatred. Some of the music is politically savvy. We have children who have a lot to say about everything in this world."

Jessica sits forward with no thought to what she is about to say. "Well, I don't want people like him dating my daughter. And the only reason you're defending him is because you probably have a son just like him at home."

Mrs. McBride, who has adjusted her hat at least three times while listening to Jessica, is face to face with her. "My son is a biologist with a Ph.D. and my daughter, who listens to this kind of music, works in the United States post office. My two children both have honorable jobs, and I've always taught them to follow their own path. Now DeShan has chosen to follow his own path, and he's making millions of dollars from all of our children. Believe me, Mrs. Jessica, you better listen to where his path is taking him because he is America's future, and your daughter, my life, and your life are somehow affected by the music this young man is putting out. I don't know how long I'm going to be sharing lodging with you people in this room, but however long it is, I want to know what everyone's philosophy is.... I'm beginning to see what yours is, Mrs. Jessica."

She turns to DeShan and loudly says, "Share the rap with us." The words resonate, and DeShan stands up hurriedly.

When DeShan starts rocking back and forth, everyone else comes to attention. As he tries to find the right beat, his dreadlocks are moving from side to side, and he makes beat box sounds with his mouth.

Jessica has her hands over her ears. Richard has taken a seat beside Jessica as though he is consoling her. Both Abu and Nantan are helping DeShan with the needed beat sounds.

> I just don't know where this life is taking me
> Drugs on the street and into my psyche.

There are times that I scream, and there are times that I cry
'Cause my life ain't jacked from the time I arrived
Ghetto life ain't no joke
It keeps me crying and searching 'cause a brother is broke
First to live and the first to die
First to vote and the first that they lie
First to come and the first to go
First to spend time in the joint and the first to electro
I just don't know where this life is taking me.
Drugs on the street and into my psyche.
I see things that a brother ain't supposed to see
Like landing on a land with brothers like me
Planting seeds that ain't for me
And then supporting a war that I don't believe
Brothers killing brothers for some shoes
Don't anyone know that we all are gonna lose
I just don't know where this life is taking me.
Drugs on the street and into my psyche.
Farming lands that you won't buy from
Spending millions on the socially elite while the brother takes a gun
Cutting forest to extend your wealth
While the rest of the country starves to death
You got the nerve to say that all we talk about is bitches and whores
While the banks of the world is controlling your minds and your stores
I just don't know where this life is taking me
Drugs on the street and into my psyche.

Richard stands up. "That's all you home boys know about is calling women bitches and whores. Maybe that's all your women are."

Jessica says, "I'm offended by your words, and every woman in any society should be offended too."

Abu says, "So are you offended by the record companies that perpetuate the stereotypes, or don't they count?"

Richard is face to face with Abu. "Don't you talk about the record companies. They're just supplying the kind of music these people want to hear."

Abu quietly asks, "How come I can't talk about the record companies? If they encouraged positive messages, children would still buy the music. It's the same way with the movies they promote in Hollywood."

Richard wants to yell at Abu, but finds it hard to do so because Abu is so calm as he talks. Richard says, "My uncles work at some of those movie studios you're talking about. They tried to make wholesome movies, but no one wanted to see them."

"How do you know no one wants to see them?" Abu asks. "I bought a ticket to see an ethnic movie, and when I looked at the stub closely, it said that I'd bought a ticket to another movie."

Abu stands back when he sees that Richard is upset and that at any second Richard might hit him.

Abu says, "Are you Jewish?"

"What kind of question is that? I'm not answering that question."

Abu says, "A question about bitches and whores is a respectable conversation, but your ethnicity isn't?"

DeShan is disturbed as he tries to respond, "You mean to tell me that you were so interested in those two little words that you didn't hear my message?"

Richard says, "The message can't be heard over those negative words. My father didn't participate in boycotts and get thrown in jail for you to use words like that."

Mrs. McBride is surprised. "You mean to tell me your family participated in boycotts? What kind of boycotts?"

Richard stands proudly and says, "My father marched with Dr.

Martin Luther King, Jr., and I am ashamed of where this movement has led to, quite frankly, drugs, killings, and children having babies."

DeShan says, "You see, you're just like everybody else. I have a message, and I share that message with other people like me who are experiencing life in the same way."

Mrs. McBride says, "Have you ever considered widening your consumer base?"

All of a sudden, there are sounds coming from the corner as "Um uma um da um" is being chanted over and over in rhythmic timing. Nantan has taken his hair out of a ponytail and is almost in a trancelike state as he continues to chant.

The room is quiet as they all sit down and listen. Five minutes pass before the chanting stops. No more words are exchanged, and even though it is the middle of the day, the ceiling slowly closes.

Chapter 23

May 12

Precious waits for her sister in the waiting area of the airport. She tries to call Jazzy on her cell phone, and Jazzy isn't answering. Finally there is a call from Jazzy saying that she is in the luggage area. She also tells Precious that she has a surprise.

Precious is excited as she waits for her sister to come through the double doors. As the door opens, though, there stands Jazzy, but she isn't alone. There standing beside her is Larry. Precious's expression changes as she watches them walk toward her.

Larry kisses her. "So, are you glad to see me?"

Precious pulls away from him and hugs her sister. Precious whispers in Jazzy's ear, "I am going to kill you." Precious turns to Larry and asks, "How long are you planning on being here?"

"Well, I was on my way to California when I saw Jazzy in the airport. She told me what was going on down here, and I decided that I needed to come check it out for myself."

"You didn't answer the question. How long are you going to be here?"

"Until you don't need me anymore, but I have to be in San Francisco in three days."

"So you're only going to be here three days then. Where are you going to stay?"

"Wherever you're staying will suffice."

Precious smiles and says to Jazzy, "Let's go to the bathroom. Larry, will you watch the luggage?"

"Yeah, sure."

Inside the bathroom Precious slams the door as she walks into the middle of the bathroom. "What the hell is Larry doing here and how come you didn't tell me he was coming with you? This is a sad occasion. Now I've got to try to entertain him on top of everything else going on."

"He got on the plane, and I tried to reach you.… I thought you would be happy to see him. He is your love, isn't he?"

"No, he is not my love. He comes around once a month, and I have no idea where he is the rest of the time. I'm sick of him. I've got too many things on my mind. I hung up on him. I thought he could take a hint and now he's down here." Precious seems to be talking to herself and her disappointment is plainly apparent to Jazzy.

"I know you're still grieving the deaths of Mom and Dad," Jazzy says, choosing her words carefully as she washes her hands. "Are you transferring your emotions to this woman?"

"Jazzy, I know what this sounds like to you, but this is different. I learned a lot from this lady since I've been in this godforsaken hot weather. I only wish that you could have had a chance to meet her."

"You talk about her like she's dead already."

"I don't know what to think, Jazzy. No one seems to know anything. I don't think these people would hesitate to kill someone down here. I got a note a few weeks ago that basically told me I should leave, and then when I didn't leave, people chased me down the road in zombie attire."

"You what? Are you all right?"

Precious nods.

"Well, no one tells a Jennings woman when she should leave. And everything is about to change. Ryan gave me the name of the police officer here as well as other names of people I should talk to. I've got some contacts here, and I promise you by tomorrow evening I'll have some information. I just need to relax tonight and eat some of your award-winning pasta."

"What are we going to do about Larry?" Precious asks.

"Well, I'm surprised. I thought you still liked him. Put his butt in the spare room and let's find Mrs. McBride."

On the way to the guesthouse, Precious starts to tell Larry and Jazzy about the dinner that night, but she decides to wait as she decides what to do.

After showering, Jazzy comes out of the guest room in a silk lounging gown. Her hair is swinging and bouncing as she walks. Jazzy could easily win a Miss Universe contest if she tried out.

Larry watches both Jazzy and Precious and thinks, *I'm in heaven.* Precious is preparing food as he tries to keep a conversation going, but finally realizes that Precious truly isn't interested anymore. She finally says, "There's a bedroom downstairs. You may take that room."

"I thought maybe I could sleep with you," Larry says hopefully.

"Well, you thought wrong. That's not going to happen anymore. I've got a lot going on, and I really don't have time to entertain you."

"I know you don't have time to entertain. I came down to help."

"Yeah, you came down to help for three days."

"Well, at least I came."

"You came after I hung up on you. Look, my sister and I are going out to the McBride family's house for dinner. I'm sure that wouldn't interest you."

"Yes, it would. What time are we going?"

Precious takes a deep breath and says, "Six o'clock."

"I'll go shower then."

For the first time in months Precious feels completely uncomfortable as she sets the salad and pasta down in front of her sister, who is dialing a number on the phone.

"Can I speak with Hal?" Precious hears her sister say. Jazzy chooses not to eat until the conversation is over.

"Hal, this is Jessica Jennings. I'm a reporter for WSOL in Michigan. I believe we have a mutual friend, Steve Kan, in Michigan?"

Jazzy laughs as the conversation goes on for ten minutes before she tells Hal why she is in town. She picks up a pencil and writes down the name and address of a restaurant and promises to be there at noon the next day.

Precious sits down next to her sister and takes a deep breath. "We are invited to dinner tonight. It will give you a chance to meet her family."

"What time are we supposed to be there? Shoot, I thought that I could just stay here and relax."

"They asked us to be there at six."

"What time is it now?"

"Four o'clock."

Jazzy looks tired as she gazes into her big sister's eyes. "Okay. I'll go, but I don't want to be there long. I wanna come back and sleep."

"Deal," Precious says, glad that she doesn't have to argue with her sister about going.

Precious, Jazzy, and Larry are on time as they mount the stairs leading to the porch. They ring the doorbell once before the door opens. There stands Wendy with another black lace veil, this one with white trim, draped about her head. Jazzy stares at Precious and is about to say, "What the hell?" when Precious says, "Have you heard anything?"

Wendy shakes her head and invites them into the mansion. Rosa has on another exquisite dress with every strand of her hair in place and invites the guests into the home. "That's a lovely dress," Precious manages to say.

"Thank you. I bought it in Paris several months ago."

Rosa's gaze goes right to Larry. He smiles charmingly at her.

Jazzy is standing there quiet as the two women exchange niceties.

"Rosa, I would like to introduce you to my sister, Jazzy. She came down to help us."

Rosa glances at Jazzy and barely says, "Hello."

Jazzy holds out her hand to shake Rosa's hand, but Rosa turns around as if Jazzy isn't good enough to shake hands with. Jazzy is about to say, "What the hell?" when Michael walks into the room.

Precious introduces Larry, adding, "He will be here for three days."

Rosa smiles and says, "Hello. How was your trip? Would you like something to drink? What do you think about this part of the country?"

Larry is about to answer when Michael comes in closer to the group.

Wendy says to Precious, "My brother here must be tired. He was up at the crack of dawn talking to people and looking for our mother. I'm so proud he is my big brother. I kinda believe that he's going to find her. He just got home a few minutes ago."

Precious smiles, trying to add levity to the room. "Well, who is cooking dinner?"

Wendy laughs and says, "Michael was going to tell you that he cooked, but Bertha did most of the cooking."

Michael comes to his own defense. "I cooked too."

Larry watches the exchange between Michael and Precious and decides to interrupt. "My name is Larry, and I'm Precious's man."

Before thinking, Precious says, "No, you're not." Precious thinks quickly. "What did you cook?"

Michael seems a little confused as he stares at Larry as he talks. He tries to make a joke. "I boiled the water."

The room explodes into laugher. Everyone is laughing except Larry and Rosa.

Michael takes Precious's hand when he is introduced to Jazzy, who watches the body language of Michael and Precious and realizes more is going on. Jazzy points to Rosa, and Precious says, "Rosa is Michael's ex-wife. She came down from LA when she heard about Mrs. McBride being kidnapped."

Jazzy once again is thinking, *What the hell?* and Precious can once again read her sister's body language.

Jazzy takes a deep breath and says to the people standing in the room, "My sister asked me to come down here to see if I can help find out what happened to your mother. This is my job—I investigate crimes and I find people—and I believe that I can help find your mother."

Michael smiles and squeezes Precious's hand as he thanks Jazzy for coming down. "If you need anything," he says, "please let me know. Tomorrow I'll introduce you to people who can help you if I'm not around. It isn't a good idea for you to be walking around by yourself."

Jazzy smiles and says, "Good deal."

Larry steps up and says, "I came down here to see about Precious. I'm concerned about her safety. She told me what happened to her."

Precious says, "Yeah, he's concerned for my safety for three days, and then he has to leave."

Michael says, "Man, you don't have to worry about her while I'm here."

"Well, is that so?" Larry says. "Were you here when people were chasing her and your mother disappeared?"

Precious says, "That was a cruel remark, even for you."

"I'm just trying to keep it real and hold on to my woman."

"I am not your woman."

Michael, sensing the tension between Larry and Precious, excuses himself and says that he is helping Bertha in the kitchen. He walks back into the kitchen, leaving Wendy, Rosa, Jazzy, Larry, and Precious in the living room.

Precious looks around at the group and decides to go into the kitchen with Michael. Bertha shakes her head and laughs as Precious enters the room. "Boy, this is more drama than I've ever seen."

"Bertha, I didn't ask for this. Honestly, I didn't," Precious says.

"I know. Believe me, I know."

Precious picks up a carrot as she says, "How are you taking all of this?"

Bertha's hands are shaking as she says, "I'm scared to death."

Michael asks, "Where's the large pan?"

Larry comes into the room, and Bertha stares at him, somehow knowing the story of his life. She doesn't say anything, but she can't take her eyes off him.

Larry says, "I came in here to tell Michael that he has a phone call, and Wendy told me to tell you to take it upstairs."

"Come on, Precious. I really need some support. Would you go with me on this one?"

Precious and Michael leave the room, heading for the private phone.

Larry frowns and turns to leave when Bertha stands in front of the door, blocking it so that he can't leave. Bertha asks him to take a seat.

"Who are you?" Bertha says to him, not allowing him to make excuses as to who he really is.

"What do you mean?"

"You go around camouflaging your true identity. You just kinda blend in to your surroundings, don't you?"

"What are you talking about?"

"I got two children like you. They don't like who they are, so they try to be something else. I haven't seen my children in years 'cause I'm Native American and proud of it. I bet you haven't had a committed relationship in your life. That poor girl in the other room has lost almost everything important to her. I wish I could tell my children to wake up before they lose everything. I'm going to say it to you, and I hope someone is saying that to my children."

Larry thinks, *Bingo. Someone I just met knows me better than I know myself, but I'll never let her know it.* Larry pulls his thoughts together and says, "Yeah, I'm mixed up. My mother is German and Italian, and my father is Black and Native American. I'm universal, and I date universally."

"Well, while you're dating universally, do you mind thinking universally as well? You can cross over the ocean and back again, and you will be no closer in finding yourself."

"How do you know I don't accept myself?"

"Because you treat women like dirt. Precious has not once said anything bad about you, but I know you aren't treating her right."

"How do you know that?"

Bertha leans in toward Larry as she says, "You should have been here on the first plane smokin' when you heard that people had been chasing her. She could have died. She was in the hospital, and to my knowledge, you didn't even call. So how can you say you care for her when you aren't even there for her?"

Larry thinks about what she has said and decides, *She doesn't know me. Who does she think she is talking to me like that? I don't have to talk to her. I'll probably never see her again.* Larry walks toward the door and says sarcastically, "Thank you for those little words of wisdom." He walks into the living room, glad to be out of the same space as Bertha.

Rosa stands up and walks to the front of the brick fireplace when Larry walks back into the room. The brick fireplace covers one side of the long living room.

Precious comes down the stairs as Rosa is about to make a speech. "I want to thank you for coming in and helping us." Rosa takes a handkerchief out of her pocket and pretends to shed tears. "I just want you ladies to know that you can report your findings to me. I'm Michael's right hand right now. I'm going to help him get through this tragedy. On behalf of the family, I would like to thank you for your concern. But you must remember to let the police do their job. You just can't go out looking in places all willy-nilly. "

Wendy, who has been quiet through Rosa's oration, lifts her veil for the first time. The fragile expression on her face is replaced with an air of total discontent and disgust as she says, "Why don't you sit down? You don't run the show in this family. You didn't even show up with your man when his father died, so you don't run nothin' here. These people are my guests, and I say they have full run of the house while they're here."

"Well," Jazzy says, "I'm beginning to get the picture."

Chapter 24

Tensions persist as the captives agonize over being locked up. They are all concerned about their fate. Disagreements surface between them. Every morning and evening, four gunmen bring food and medicine in while four additional gunmen wait at the door. It has become a ritual. Faces are covered and guns are drawn. Someone in the group always asks the gunmen what is going to happen to them. Even though the gunmen brought Mrs. McBride a hat, not one has been friendly enough to talk to. The only time the group sees some sunlight now is when the gunmen open the door.

Jessica has tried to seduce several of the gunmen, but because of their masks, change of clothes and shoes, she isn't sure which one she is talking to. This strategy has failed for her and the group. Mrs. McBride has tried to reason with them, and this hasn't worked either. Richard has tried the intellectual approach and is using deductive reasoning with them, but this hasn't worked either.

Although Mrs. McBride is taking her medication, she is becoming weaker. She masks her illness by showing strong leadership and is only showing her pain when the roof is shut tight and no one can see her. For the last three days the roof has been closed. The arguments are nonstop every day. Mrs. McBride doesn't have the strength to stop the quarrels, and even though no one is admitting it, the disputes have made their situation even worse. The environment is gloomy, and the dissension has sickened everyone in the group to some degree.

Every moment of the day someone is saying something negative and unhealthy about someone else. Richard, who has lost all composure, calls Abu, DeShan, and Nantan names. Jessica and DeShan are constantly arguing. The surroundings continue to lend themselves to manipulation of feelings.

Today, DeShan, who feels the deprivation of light and not being around his friends and family, shares his true feelings with the group. "I have never been confined before, but this feels like being in jail, in seclusion with a lot of other people who don't know me and care little to nothing about me."

Richard laughs sarcastically and says, "You should know all about that."

"What are you talkin' about, man?" DeShan says, wishing he hadn't uttered the words.

"Oh, nothing. I just wondered why you haven't been in jail. All Black men go to jail."

DeShan waves his hand in Richard's direction. "Man, you are stupid." This surprises Richard.

Abu walks over and calmly says, "Maybe I'm wrong, because a Jewish person would never own a cattle farm. They think they are too good to raise cattle. Jewish people talk a certain way, and I don't hear that in your voice."

DeShan tells Abu that he is stupid too. "Most of the Jews in the Bible own cattle. What is it with you and Richard anyway?"

Richard says, "What is it with you and the Jewish thing? You've been trying to call me Jewish ever since I made that remark about movies. Man, you're the stupid one."

Jessica says, "All you men are stupid. You can't even get us out of here. Bunch of dim-witted, cowardly boys fighting over what ethnicity you're from. What the hell does it matter if we aren't going to get out of this situation? You're a bunch of stupid, idiotic morons."

Those words are irritating and resonating in Richard's head. He forgets that there are other people in the room as he says to Jessica, "Well, that's a lot of names coming out of a woman who is fridged."

"Just because I won't have sex with you, you call me fridged? I would rather have sex with a one-eyed Kobold monster—you know those small creatures that are very old and wrinkled and all they want is scraps from the dinner table? You are a morsel of a man."

Richard says, "You must be talking about your ex-husband."

DeShan pipes in, "No, she was talking about your mama."

Jessica turns to DeShan and says, "No, I'm talking about your mother. She musta been on some crazy damn drugs when she had you."

DeShan says, "Well, at least I had a mother. Yours is a six-eyed gnome."

Jessica is in DeShan's face. "Well, at least she could see."

Mrs. McBride, with all the power she has left, stomps her feet as she is sitting in the corner of the room gasping for air.

Nantan starts another Native-American chant, and everyone's attention is averted from bickering as they focus their anger on Nantan. They're sick of hearing the chants and have told Nantan several times.

In addition to the chanting, their irritation is directed toward the environment. The air isn't circulating, and everyone is wishing that the roof would retract for at least ten minutes today, but this hasn't happened in a while.

For the past three days, the quarreling has been severe enough that everyone now knows what emotional abuse feels like. No one is speaking civilly to anyone.

Richard pushes Jessica into a nearby wall.

DeShan says, "Hey, man, leave her alone. I know she's hell to deal with, but why don't you pick on someone your own size?"

Richard turns to DeShan and says, "I think I will."

Richard hits DeShan and sends him flying across the room. DeShan is back within a flash, tackling Richard, sending him to the floor.

Jessica is on Richard's back, hitting him as hard as she can. Abu tries to break the fight up and is punched by Richard. Abu asks, "Why did you hit me?"

"'Cause I've never liked you," is Richard's only reply.

Abu gives Richard one good hit, sending Richard to the floor. DeShan hits Abu. This stuns Abu as he asks, "Why did you hit me?"

DeShan says rather perplexed, "Because I wanted to be the one to knock him down."

Abu says, "Well, in that case, why don't I knock you down, and the two of you can start from scratch."

Abu pushes DeShan, and the two of them exchange punches. Jessica, not knowing whom she likes the least, decides to punch both DeShan and Abu. Richard is recovering from his punch and jumps back into the group. Fists are flying everywhere. Richard is able to get his hands around Abu's neck, and DeShan is forcing Richard's head away from Abu. Jessica is on DeShan's back, punching him wildly.

Unexpectedly, the door flies open, and there stand eight gunmen who are watching the skirmish. They begin to laugh so hard they almost drop their guns. This goes on for over five minutes as several guns are drawn on the captives. Several of the gunmen fall to the floor. Their amusement seems to be a paralyzing force to the captives. The laughter sends spine-tingling chills through the captives as the gunmen delight in watching their heavens collide. Each boxer falls to the floor and away from the others as the gunmen continue to cackle hysterically.

Richard, DeShan, and Abu plunge toward the gunmen. The laughter stops as guns are drawn. All three men step back as the gunmen's fingers are on the triggers.

One steps forward and says, "Because you have all that energy, you won't be receiving dinner nor medicine tonight."

After saying that, all eight gunmen leave the room without another word.

In a weak voice, Mrs. McBride says to the group, "This cannot go on."

Richard stands up and says cattily, "I'm not going to be anyone's entertainment."

DeShan agrees, then says, "We've got to figure out how to work together. We've got all these great minds in this one room. We've got to try to work together to get ourselves out of this situation."

Nantan starts a chant in the corner of the room until Richard tells him to shut the hell up.

Mrs. McBride says, "This has got to stop, and it's got to stop now."

DeShan stands up, too, as he says, "Yeah, let's figure out how to overthrow these guys and take their guns."

Jessica stands up and says, "We have no weapons to fight with, you moron."

Richard says, "You mean you called us cowards because we refuse to take these criminals out without guns? You're the only moron in the group, Jessica."

Abu, who is sitting down, tired from the fight, now stands and, for the first time, there is excitement in his voice. "We have Mrs. McBride's needles."

"No, we don't," Mrs. McBride says. "Aren't you paying attention? They've always asked for the needles back. I have no needles. We have no weapons."

Nantan, the only person who has not joined the group, sits quietly on the floor. "I've been thinking about this. They've given Mrs. McBride just enough insulin to keep her alive."

Mrs. McBride says, "What they have given me is not enough. I'm getting weaker because of it." She has decided not to complain and changes the subject. "We have all these fine minds in one room. I was thinking—just thinking—you hear me?" She moves in closer to the group while sifting through her thoughts. "I believe that there are people out there somewhere looking for us and, knowing my son, I believe that we'll be found really soon. Now … um … we have so many groups behind us—environmental, economic, organic farmers, Black farmers—what if we got together as a united group and demand changes once we get out of here? Our voices would have to be heard."

DeShan leans closer to Mrs. McBride and says, "What kind of changes are we going to make, and who are we going to make these changes for, and what difference does it make if we're never getting out of here?"

"Listen, DeShan, you've got to open your mind. We're going to get out of here. Don't you know if they wanted to kill us they would have done so a long time ago?" Mrs. McBride, sensing that she has everyone's attention, says, "If we can get out of here, we're going to start thinking about how to save the rest of the world, and then we're going to make changes to the world we're living in, and it's going to start with us. In order for these changes to work, we've got to work together as a group. If we can't work together, we won't be able to change the world, and we shall die together."

DeShan, who is standing beside Mrs. McBride, asks, "Is anybody courageous enough to work together? We've been really unintelligent by separating ourselves. Let's try working together."

Richard walks toward Mrs. McBride and DeShan and says, "I'm in."

Mrs. McBride and everyone else in the room are shocked but rather pleased with his response, so Mrs. McBride says, "What made you change your mind, Richard?"

"I've always wanted to work together. I just felt as though I had to fend off attackers. Everyone's anger has been directed toward me."

Mrs. McBride says, "So you're going to help with the changes?"

"I will."

Jessica and Abu raise their hands and both say, "Me too."

Nantan, who is still sitting on the floor, says, "What about getting out of here?"

Mrs. McBride says, "We'll get out of here, and when we do, we'll have a united voice. How about it, Nantan. Are you interested?"

Nantan slowly gets out of his comfortable position and joins the group. Peacefully he says, "I'm in."

Mrs. McBride extends her hand and, one by one, each person places his hand on top of the hand below it. When all hands are stacked, they all look around at each other and smile. This is the first time everyone has smiled at the same time.

As the group starts to laugh, one half of the roof starts to retract. Sunlight pours in. It's the most sunlight the group has gotten in their time in the dungeon.

Chapter 25

Rosa walks around the McBride mansion with a cup of coffee and a saucer in her hand. Her mind is racing as she decides her next move. She walks up the stairs and into Mrs. McBride's room, searching for any legal documents. She has turned the room upside down before realizing the safe is at the end of the walk-in closet. She tries to open it, and it doesn't budge. She tries several more times before realizing that the safe will not open for her. She makes a phone call before heading back downstairs.

It is seven o'clock in the morning, and she is flawlessly dressed. She has rented a car, and it sits in front of the mansion. She is careful not to get any of the coffee on her pink suit.

Michael comes downstairs, heading out the door. Rosa smiles and asks, "Where are you going?"

"I'm taking Jazzy over to Mr. Lane's house. I don't know when I'll be back."

Rosa shifts feet as she says, "Oh, I forgot to tell you. Jazzy already called this morning. She told me to tell you that she's running late and won't be ready for another hour."

Michael stops. He is about to leave the house. "I didn't hear the phone ring this morning."

Rosa is cool as she sips her coffee. "Well, you musta been in the shower when she called."

Michael walks over to the phone. "I'll call her."

Rosa doesn't move as her posture shows her level of confidence. "You can call if you want to. She and that sister of hers said that they were going out for a morning jog." Rosa takes another sip and says, "That will give us just enough time for a quickie."

Michael picks up the phone and calls Mr. Lane. Rosa moves to a seat close to him. Michael realizes that he has to respond to her suggestion of a quickie.

Michael smiles as he starts to hang up the phone, choosing to play with it before placing it back on the receiver. "As tempting as that sounds, I think I need to shovel manure in the barn. Give Jazzy my cell phone number when she calls."

"How can I give her the number when I don't even know it?"

Rosa is so close to Michael that he is having a difficult time breathing. "Oh, okay. I'll call Precious in an hour."

"What is your cell phone number?"

"Baby, you don't need the number. We see each other here."

With that, Michael is out of the house as fast as he can move, not allowing Rosa to ask any more questions.

Rosa watches as Michael walks toward the barn. Rosa then calls out to Bertha, who comes downstairs in her gown.

"Bertha, I need you to go over to the pharmacy for me. I'm not feeling well, and I need the products on this list." Rosa slumps over in the chair as she wipes her forehead with a tissue.

Bertha looks intently at Rosa and says, "How long are you going to be in Mrs. McBride's home?"

"I'll be glad to talk to you about that when you return from the pharmacy. Please take my car."

Rosa holds up the keys with one hand while dabbing her head with the other hand.

"I'll go for you today. I'm only doing this for the family. Please don't ask me to do anything else for you. I don't work for you."

"Thank you. I'll keep that in mind before I ask you to do anything else for me."

Rosa is impatient waiting for Bertha to get dressed. Finally Bertha walks out of the front door. Rosa watches as Bertha pulls out of the driveway. She then looks at her watch. Rosa waits eagerly for her guest to arrive. She paces the living room several times before heading out of the house. She goes out to the barn and peeks in on Michael. He is shoveling hay, and it seems as though he has just started this task.

As Rosa walks back to the house, a truck pulls up. It reads ROGER'S KEYS. Rosa rushes the man up the stairs and into Mrs. McBride's room. He has the safe open in fifteen minutes. Rosa hands him money and rushes him out the door. She goes back upstairs to go through the documents in Mrs. McBride's safe. She reads several bank statements before heading downstairs again.

Rosa is dancing in the living room when Bertha comes back home from the pharmacy. She is stunned to see Rosa frolicking around the room.

"Bertha, I feel so much better. I've got to go downtown. Could I have the keys?"

Bertha, who isn't saying anything, hands her the keys and the bag, which reads DOLMAN'S PHARMACY. "Remember, Rosa, don't ask me to do anything else for you. I don't know what you're up to, but I will not be a part of it, and I'll be watching you closely. Dancing around Mrs. McBride's house like you own it."

"Don't be silly, Bertha. I have nothing to hide. I'll be back shortly." She collects the car keys and heads toward her rental car.

It only takes Rosa five minutes to drive into the small town. She spies the police department right away and pulls in front of the door. She applies more lipstick and checks her appearance in the small overhead mirror. She spies several people playing checkers in front of the police department. She is cordial to the men as she walks past them.

There inside the police department is Wilbert. She notices that he is the only person in the office. "Can I speak to the man in charge of this police department?"

Wilbert, who is about six feet tall and almost six feet wide, answers Rosa over a puff of his cigar while sorting through mail. "That would be me," he says without looking up.

"I'm here in town to support my ex-husband. He's trying to find his mother, Mrs. McBride."

Wilbert smirks a little as she says Mrs. McBride's name.

Rosa walks over to the desk and sits on top of it while raising her skirt. It has elevated up to mid-thigh. Her legs are large and shapely as she crosses them while lighting a cigarette.

Wilbert, who is reading a letter, doesn't look up until he smells smoke. When he does look up, he is staring at Rosa's long legs. He gawks several seconds before walking over to where she is sitting. He is standing over her, face to face, when he says, "Please don't smoke in here."

Rosa says, "You are smoking."

Wilbert says, "That's because I am the boss and I make up the rules."

Rosa blows smoke into his face before putting the cigarette out. Wilbert looks out the window, then walks over to the door and locks it. He walks over to the window and pulls the blinds down. He then walks back over to Rosa. He is standing in front of her as he says, "What do you want here?"

Rosa smiles deviously as she says, "I need your help."

Wilbert, who is wildly amused, asks seductively, while wiping a fly off her breast, "How can I help you?"

"Well, you and your men are out trying to find Mrs. McBride, aren't you?"

"Why, yes. I've got men out working with the FBI right now."

"Well," says Rosa, fondling Wilbert's shirt passionately, "I don't want you to find her."

"What's in it for me if we don't?"

Rosa whispers in his ear, and Wilbert is now more interested in her bribe.

"I'll see what I can do," he says, placing both hands on her hips. "I'll meet you at the Hotel Ann in Columbus, but as fine as you are, I need something more than that. How about if we talk tonight at the hotel about how much you're willing to pay me not to find her?"

"When you can get them to stop working on the case, call me, and I'll meet you at Hotel Ann in Columbus, and I might pay you then."

"Well, I wanna know what I'm getting myself into. I wanna meet you tonight, and I want half of the money tonight."

He touches her in her secret place before she answers, "Okay, I'll meet you tonight, but you'll only get half of me and half of the money, and I want to be discreet."

"Honey, I'm going to be cautious 'cause I'm married. You just be there tonight, and I'll get these people out of here real soon. You just make sure you're there tonight with the money."

Rosa stands real close to him and whispers, "I will."

Chapter 26

Sunbeams flow through the dungeon-like area. The roof has been completely retracted and gunmen are sitting around the edge of the open roof. Energy is pouring into the room. There is laughter as the captives work together preparing documents to take to the United Nations concerning the state of the Earth. The captives have been allowed paper and pencils. Jessica is sprawled out on the dirty linoleum floor, happier than she has been in years. She has papers all around her, sorting through them and categorizing them according to their importance.

Mrs. McBride thinks, *What a fine group of people when we are working together.*

Jessica is excited as she writes down what is being said. No one is noticing Mrs. McBride, who seems weaker by the day. Perspiration is falling down her face, but it is masked by her excitement.

"Do you think we will ever be allowed to leave this room?" Abu says while sharing detailed information with the group about the economy and the world's wealth.

All eyes are on Mrs. McBride, who seems to understand how their captors think. "I've been thinking and studying this situation." She takes in a mouthful of air and breathes out before saying, "Do you see what's going on around us? We're working together as a group. When we are fighting, the roof is closed completely. When we are working together, we get sunshine. I feel as though we are mice in a maze—we ring a bell and get rewarded. I'm beginning to see why they brought us together. Believe it or not, they've brought together some of the brightest minds in the world. I think they wanted us to work together from the beginning. I don't know about the rest of you, but I've been in the dark long enough. Now I want sunshine. I don't want to argue, and I don't want you to bicker either. I'm enjoying the glow."

Time is passing fast as the group tries to recall important information about their research while complaining about not having books and access to the Internet. Mrs. McBride is stretched out on the floor with her hat over her face. Hours go by and everyone is working hard, writing and talking about their findings.

DeShan is watching Mrs. McBride intently, observing her unusual behavior. He takes a seat beside her and waits for her to wake up, and her waking up doesn't happen. DeShan picks up Mrs. McBride's hand, and it goes limp. DeShan stands up slowly as he says, "There's something wrong with Mrs. M."

Everyone stops what they are doing and crowds around her, first trying to shake her and then checking for vital signs. Nantan says, "She's alive. She's just unconscious. We've got to get the gunmen's attention. She needs a doctor."

Richard, Jessica, and Abu knock on the door, trying to get their attention any way they can. They try shouting to the gunmen on the roof, but are unable to get their attention.

Nantan turns to DeShan and says, "DeShan, get me a wet cloth. Mrs. McBride, hang in there. We're not going to let anything happen to you. Hang on."

It takes fifteen minutes of constant pounding on the door before several gunmen in masks enter the room.

"What do you want?" The voice sounds as though it has an accent.

Nantan says nervously, "There's something wrong with Mrs. McBride. We can't wake her up."

One gunman says to the other, "Get the doctor."

With guns still drawn, the remaining gunmen order the captives to line up against the wall with their backs to Mrs. McBride. They then tell the captives to put their hands on their heads.

It takes five minutes before another man enters the dungeon with a medical bag. One hour later, Mrs. McBride is sitting up wondering what happened. Even though the gunmen are still holding guns on the hostages, the captives can tell that Mrs. McBride is better. All the hostages wonder if the guards will take her out and put her in the hospital where she should be.

They hear Mrs. McBride say, "Stop all the fuss." The guards try to take her away, but she refuses to leave without the other hostages.

She is standing wobbly as she says to them, "This isn't a suitable place for anyone. Tell me right now, when will we be leaving this godforsaken place?"

The gunman who seems to be the spokesman says, "Relax. Lady, you're going with us, and the rest will be free in a matter of days."

Mrs. McBride is on her feet now asking, "How many days?"

"I don't know, but it will be soon."

"Well, it wouldn't look so good for you if I died in this place, now would it? On top of kidnapping, you'd also be faced with murder."

The gunmen are confused about what they should do.

"Lady, you're going with us."

"No, I won't unless the others are released with me."

"Well, suit yourself. I can't tell you when you'll get out of here, and you need to be in the hospital."

"My friends need to be able to leave this place and move forward with their own lives too, and you won't let that happen. I'll stay here until we all are free or I'll die right here."

When the gunmen leave the room, the captives crowd around Mrs. McBride. Although they are concerned about Mrs. McBride's health, the solidarity she has shown has only brought the group closer. They each wonder if, given the same situation, they would have made the decision to stay. The camaraderie is now strong as they decide what needs to be done next.

Mrs. McBride, realizing the closeness of the group, calls Nantan over to sit next to her. "Tell me a legend regarding your people."

He smiles and says, "I'll be glad to do this. This is the legend from the Archives of Blue Panther." Nantan takes a deep breath and verbalizes the myth that has been passed down through six generations. "This is entitled Caddo, Sacred Medicine Water. Once the favor of the Great Spirit rested on the abundant forest, flowers, songbirds, and small animals of these quiet hills. Then a fierce dragon devastated the land, bringing disease and hunger on the people. The Indian nations pleaded with the Great Spirit to subdue the dragon, and the might of all the heavenly forces contrived to bury it deep under the mountain, where it shakes the earth even today. Once the Great Spirit had reclaimed his beautiful resting spot, he caused pure water to gush from the earth and asked that its favorite place be held in neutral ground, so all can share in the healing waters."

Nantan looks around at the group and expresses his genuine feelings. "I am so proud of Mrs. McBride. She has the Great Spirit in her. She could have left us, and she would have had every right to, but she didn't, and we learned that we will be getting out of here soon. She is truly our pure water."

Nantan changes the direction of his legend by saying, "I went to your universities to learn what you people know about the earth and her waters. I ended up teaching others what was passed down to me from my ancestors. If we don't make changes in the way we live, the air won't be safe for us to breathe, and there will be no clean water for our children to drink. I believe that the Great Sprit brought us together to solve some of these problems."

DeShan, who is working on another rap, bounces around the room showing his solidarity to the group.

Richard, who is sitting pensively, now stands, "I have something I need to say." Everyone is noticing the seriousness in his eyes. "Abu is right, kinda, I … um … am Jewish. My mother is Swedish and my father is half Jewish—his mother was Jewish. He stopped following the Jewish faith when he met my mother; his family disowned him. He believed in freedom and what Dr. King preached, but he wanted to be known as a White person. He taught that to me, and all I want to be known as is a White man. He settled in Nebraska and decided to farm, so I became a farmer too. I don't know how Abu knew who I was. I've been denying this all my life. This is the first time I've ever admitted it."

Mrs. McBride thinks for a while. "So what are you going to do differently?"

Richard thinks. "I think I'll try to learn more about all sides of me and my family. I don't know, but one day I might go spend time with my father's family."

Abu smiles. "Well, you know that my people don't like your people."

Richard smiles back. "I do know about that and, secretly, I didn't like you until I got to know you. You're all right."

Mrs. McBride says, "Well this is about more than just the state of the Earth. It's about the state of our psyche as well." Mrs. McBride hits the wall while replying to the group. "Are we almost ready with the state of the Earth address, Jessica?"

Jessica is still writing on the floor. "I just have to add a couple of pieces to our work and then I'll be finished."

Mrs. McBride states, "Take your time. I don't know how long these people will hold us here."

Richard looks up at the open air. The glass ceiling has been retracted. "Well, if you're right, Mrs. McBride, that every time we work for the good of the group the roof coils back, they may let us out of here soon. If not, that's our way out." He points to the ceiling.

DeShan looks up, smiling. "The way out is up."

Chapter 27

Michael introduces Jazzy to Mr. Lane and his son, Glen. "Make sure you have one of them with you at all times when you're asking questions in this town."

Jazzy shakes her head. This is the fifth time Michael has said this in the last half hour. "I promise that I'll have one of you guys with me." *Besides, Glen is a fine-looking brother. I'll be sure to have him around.* Jazzy then thinks about her fiancé and thinks, *But I can't wait to get back home to the man I love, Charles.*

Jazzy glances back at her notes. "I need to talk with the FBI and the local police department first. Regrettably, the FBI took off for Atlanta. They think for some reason that Mrs. McBride was taken there. I don't get it. All the evidence I have says that they're somewhere close to this state. I'm going back to the police department. I have some questions that need answers."

"I'll take you," Glen says, excited about being assigned to watch over Jazzy.

"Well, can we get going right away? I have a strange feeling about this case, and the quicker we get it solved, the better off I think we're going to be."

Just then Kevin, who had decided not to join the FBI in Atlanta, walks in. "I just talked with Ryan and he believes that all the kidnap victims are together somewhere in Mississippi. He also believes that DeShan is with the other kidnap victims."

Jazzy says to Michael, who had never met Kevin, "Kevin is a friend of my cousin Ryan. They both are police officers in Michigan. Ryan sent Kevin down here to watch Precious. Kevin has agreed to help us. He has already talked to the police, and he'll be the inside person for us."

Michael says, "Nice to meet you, man. Let me know how we can make your stay down here comfortable." He then turns to Jazzy and says, "I agree. But as much as possible, I'm going to be with you."

"No," Jazzy says, "you're too close to this case. I'm concerned about your emotions flaring up. I need to make sure I don't miss anything. If you were with me, I would be too worried about what you were going to say or afraid of hurting your feelings. Precious told me that you're a hothead."

Michael is angry as he shouts, "I'm not a hothead. I want to find my mother, now."

Jazzy knows that he is not going to back down. "Okay. There's this farm over toward Columbus. I hear they've been complaining about an enormous number of cars coming and going down this dirt road. The activities just started two months ago, and no one will tell me why. Maybe you can drive over there and talk to the people there." Jazzy thinks, *This should get Michael out of town for a while so that Kevin and I can work on this case.*

After writing the address down, Michael says, "I'll be in touch later today."

Michael and Precious drive down MS-12, maneuvering toward a small town outside of Columbus, Mississippi. Even though their dispositions are despondent, they are glad to be together in this heart-breaking situation. At first Precious says nothing while trying to give Michael a chance to talk about his feelings, but the quiet moments in the car with him only bring on more quiet and disturbing thoughts.

Finally Precious turns on a jazz station and A. Ray Fuller is picking "Free Spirit" on his electric guitar. Precious starts swaying in the car to the music. The music gets really good to her as she turns up the volume. She starts tapping her foot while nodding her head. Her arms are swaying as if she is about to take off in flight. Michael watches her movement and, before he realizes it, he is moving to the music too. They are driving down the highway dancing while people pass by gazing into Michael's truck, shaking their heads in disgust. Precious and Michael laugh and continue to dance to the music.

After the song ends, Michael says, "What happened to your boyfriend from Michigan?"

Precious is about to dance to Kirk Whalum's "I'll Make Love to You" when the question is asked.

"Do you know that my so-called boyfriend came to my parents' funerals and I didn't even know he was there?"

"What do you mean? Your boyfriend whom you love wasn't there to comfort you?"

"No. He just told me he was there when we talked later."

Michael starts smiling. Precious hasn't seen him smile in a while, so she decides to tell him more.

"We were on a picnic together, and we were eating fried chicken, and he insisted on eating it with a knife and fork."

Michael starts laughing harder, so Precious decides to share more information with him. "He tells me after we've gone out together that he's going to call me. Sometimes he doesn't call for a month."

"Oh, don't tell me you fall for that. How often does that happen?"

Precious wonders to herself whether she should share any more information with him or not. She finally says, "It happens all the time."

With that, Michael is laughing so hard he is having trouble seeing the road. When he finally stops laughing, he says, "I don't believe as smart as you appear that you would allow anybody to do that to you."

Precious turns to Michael and says, "Well, since I was so honest with you, tell me why of all the women in the world, you chose Rosa."

Michael stops laughing.

"Oh, it ain't so funny now, hmm?"

Michael says, "I thought she could help me get to the place I wanted to be."

"And what place was that?"

"On top of the world. You see, she and I attended the same universities. She was at the top in her class, and I was at the top in my profession. She … um … she told me she was pregnant."

When Michael says this, Precious starts laughing. "And you believed her, did you?"

"I didn't have any reason not to believe her. I married her right away. No child of mine was going to be without a father."

Precious thinks about it and starts laughing as hard as Michael laughed at her. "So when did you find out she wasn't having a baby?"

"Shortly after we got married. She didn't even act like she had a miscarriage. She just told me it was a mistake. It was a mistake all right."

Precious starts laughing again. "You fell for the oops mistake, did you now?"

"Yeah, I did." When Michael thinks about it, he starts laughing too.

Precious says, "You know you aren't in any position to talk about me, don't you?"

"Yep. I haven't made good choices either." Michael is grateful for the opportunity to talk about something other than his mother's disappearance. "So, Precious, what do you want?"

"What do you mean, what do I want?"

"I mean, what do you want in your man?"

"It's simple. I just want to be respected. I'm going to respect the person I'm with, and I want him to do the same. I fell out of love with Larry because he didn't respect me. He should have called me while I was here. He didn't."

"He came to you though."

"He came because I told him I was through with him. That's the only reason he came. When his three days were up, he got back on the plane and left. I don't know when I will see him again, if ever, and all he had to do was simply call me."

Precious holds the map in her hand as she points to the street to turn on.

"I'll do all the talking," Michael says in a deep, strong voice. "You take the mental notes."

Precious turns to Michael and says, "Michael, I know that you're worried about your mother, and I don't blame you. I got you on this, but I'll be asking questions, too, if you aren't asking the right ones."

"You don't understand these people down here." Michael momentarily takes his hands off the wheel to express how he feels.

"Oh, I understand them all right. I'm in advertising, remember?"

Michael makes another turn into a driveway, and there stands a small house that seems to be falling apart. The wood on the home, which probably was once a deep brown, has turned gray, and the screen door is falling off the hinges. Michael gives Precious another glare before getting out of the truck. He walks around to open the door for Precious. A little more relieved, Precious walks with authority toward the front door.

Michael manages to walk ahead of her and knock on the door before Precious has a chance to mount the steps to the house.

An unshaved White man in overalls who is about forty-five years old with a toothpick in his mouth comes out of the door. He gives Michael and Precious a long stare before speaking. "What do y'all want?"

Michael speaks politely. "I understand from the police and FBI that there are some strange activities going on around here."

Precious steps up and stands by Michael's side. "We lost a loved one several weeks ago, and we're just looking for any leads."

The man still doesn't say anything.

Michael then says, "We just wanna know what you know so that we can check it out for ourselves."

Finally the man says, "I told the authorities all I know." He turns to go back into the house, but Michael puts his foot on the screen door, preventing the man from going back in.

"Boy, you better get yo' damn foot off my door and get the hell out of here."

"I'm not trying to cause any problems," Michael says. "They have my mother, and she's sick. I'm just trying to get my mother back … before … something happens to her." Michael is close to tears.

The man takes the toothpick out of his mouth and scratches the back of his head. He walks out into the yard. Precious spies several abandoned cars that have rusted out and a barn that appears dangerously unsafe.

The man takes his time. "Down there, ain't supposed to be nobody living down there, but I hear cars goin' down there all times of the day and night."

Michael and Precious stare down the dirt road, weighing thoughts about traveling down the dead end.

"I'm going to take you home," Michael says, turning to Precious.

"I want to go with you."

Michael turns to the man, who is still standing there looking down the road. "What did the police find?"

"They didn't find nothin' down there. They think teenagers are using that road 'cause they found a heap of beer bottles down there. I tried to tell them that I've seen some expensive cars go down that there road."

Precious, who is still looking down the dirt road, says, "Do you think it was the Knights of Darkness?"

"I'm in the Knights of Darkness. We went down there and couldn't find nothin'."

Michael puts his arm around Precious's shoulder and says, "Thanks for the information."

The man puts the toothpick back into his mouth and says nothing more.

"Let's go down there," Precious says. Michael has plans to do that after he takes Precious back home. He admires her strength and knows that she's determined to go with him, so he decides to drive down the dirt road to check it out and then leave and bring men out to the site tomorrow. The area is wooded and ends at a long cornfield. A wood fence separates the road from the field.

"Well," Precious says, "choose. Do you want to go into the field or the woods?"

"Let's see what's going on in these woods."

Precious wishes she hadn't worn her stilettos. Michael goes into the back of the truck and brings out a pair of his old boots and shoves them into her hands.

She puts them on and finds that they are too big, but manages to keep up with him. They find beer cans in the woods that seem to lead down a path.

The day is slipping into night, and the flashlight that Michael has taken isn't giving them much hope.

Michael says, "Come on. Let's go home. I'll come back out here tomorrow with Glen and Mr. Lane.

Precious says, "This area feels weird to me. I can't explain it."

Michael takes Precious's arm while saying, "It does to me too."

They silently walk back to the car.

Michael keeps gazing into his rearview mirror, hoping to find some traces of his mother. Several times Precious has had to tell him when the truck is veering off the dirt road. At the stop sign, Michael is still staring into the rearview mirror, still looking for any clues.

Precious observes Rosa driving down the highway. Precious takes a real good look at her, even though night is falling. She knows that Rosa is driving the car, going toward Columbus.

"So, Michael, what do you and Rosa have up for tonight?"

Michael takes his eyes off the rearview mirror and watches the flow of traffic. "What did you say?"

"What do you and Rosa have up for tonight?"

"Nothing, never, and it's time to tell her to go home."

Chapter 28

Jessica, DeShan, and Richard pound on the door. They've been pounding for two hours, and no one has answered their call. The surroundings feel strange to the hostages. In the past they've heard cars outside and sometimes talking.

In the past when the hostages have knocked on the door for long periods of time, there has been an answer, but not this time. The captives thought it was unusual when the gunmen brought fifty peanut butter and jelly sandwiches and insulin for Mrs. McBride the day before with instructions not to eat all of the sandwiches at one time.

Mrs. McBride is slumped over in the corner of the room using both walls to support her weight. DeShan walks over and puts his arms around her. "Would you like some water?"

Mrs. McBride struggles to speak. "No, I'm all right. Have you heard anyone outside yet?"

"No, but they should be back soon. I mean, these sandwiches won't last that long."

Mrs. McBride struggles a little before asking DeShan to hand her paper and pencil. He hands them to her, and she starts to write.

DeShan hands Mrs. McBride a Styrofoam cup with water in it. He feels helpless in trying to alleviate some of her pain. He takes off his shirt and places it behind her head. She just smiles as she continues to write.

Abu and Richard take a seat close to Mrs. McBride as the others come in closer. Abu says, "I think they left."

Jessica asks, "Why would they just leave like that?"

Richard stares around the room before answering the question. "They got in too deep. I don't think they expected Mrs. McBride to get sick."

Jessica asks, "Well, how come they didn't release us?"

DeShan says, "They know that they're going to be in a lot of trouble. They didn't want to hang around for that."

Abu says, "Well, we've got to get out of here soon, or else we're all going to die."

Mrs. McBride is quiet as she continues to write. She has relinquished her role as leader as she waits for someone to step up to become the new leader.

DeShan, sensing her challenge, steps up and says, "Our only chance is to keep banging on the door."

He looks at the sky where the ceiling has been retracted. "We've got to figure out how to get out through the ceiling." DeShan turns to Mrs. McBride and says, "Don't worry, Mrs. M. I'm going to get you out of here alive."

She doesn't look up and continues to write.

DeShan sits up straight. "We have two primary responsibilities as I see it. The first concern is the most crucial one, and that's getting out of here and getting Mrs. M. to a hospital. Does everyone agree with that?"

All heads nod. "Next, we're going to take our findings to the United Nations. No one is going to stop us from doing that. Are we all together on this?"

All heads nod one more time. DeShan goes on, feeling more

comfortable being in a leadership position as he smiles at everyone. "Anybody know how we can get out of here?"

Richard stands up. "Well, the way I see it is the ceiling is about twenty-five feet. We don't have anything to stand on. They were clever in not putting anything in this room. How about forming a human ladder? Jessica will be at the top, and we can try to hoist her out of here."

DeShan thinks about it. "That might not be such a good idea. It appears from the trees that we could be in a forest somewhere. I don't want her out there unprotected. I suggest that we put Nantan up there. You know your way around, don't you?"

Bravely Nantan says, "Yes. I could find my way out of here."

DeShan then says, "Well, it's pretty late now. The first thing tomorrow morning, we'll get you out of here." DeShan smiles and says, "We'll give you some of these peanut butter sandwiches, and you can use them as bread crumbs." The group laughs. This seems to reduce some of the tension.

DeShan continues, "Who should be the spokesperson for the United Nations visit?"

Jessica, who has been listening, says, "I'd like to nominate DeShan and Nantan."

Abu says, "Yeah … yeah, I think that would be a good combination."

DeShan can't believe his ears. "You mean you want me to represent the group?"

Jessica then says, "You create such interesting raps. Your thinking is really fast. You've absorbed everything you've learned here, and I'm sorry I said those things about your mother. I'm sure she must be a good person." They all laugh as she speaks those words. She goes on more seriously. "I attacked you more than anyone else. You're the one I've been most scared of, and you've been the bravest. Nantan's name means 'spoken man,' and so he should go too. He's been brave in his own way. He and Mrs. McBride were smart enough not to get involved in our fighting. What does everyone else think?"

Abu is glad he doesn't have to go and says, "I agree. I was going to go, but I really didn't want to."

Richard stands within the circle, feeling a little miffed. "I would have liked to have been the spokesperson of the group. I have more skills than anyone else to talk effectively to the powers that be."

Abu says softly, "You've just come to terms with yourself. You have other things to work out right now."

Richard is a little infuriated as he sits down.

Mrs. McBride stops writing and puts down her pencil.

"Hey, Mrs. M., when are you gonna share your writings with us?" DeShan asks, trying to include her in the conversation.

She straightens up her hat. "I agree that Nantan and DeShan should be the two to represent the captives. I think they would do a good job. Richard, you'll be there. None of us will go to the United Nations until you've made amends with your family. Find yourself first. That's more important than speaking out. Speak within first."

DeShan is glad that Mrs. McBride is in agreement. "So, are you going to read what you've been writing or what?"

The other captives wait for her answer. Noticing the attention that is focused on her, she states loudly and clearly, "Now is the time to share my thoughts with you. I know that there are people out there looking for us, and don't you forget it and don't you give up."

"Is that it?" DeShan asks Mrs. McBride.

"No, that isn't it."

Mrs. McBride pulls herself up with the help of DeShan and Richard. She straightens out her dress, one that she has worn for the past two weeks. Realizing that her words need to encourage hope—hope that she is losing every day—she smiles as she looks around the room at the others. Even though she can barely stand, she stands proudly. All eyes are on her, and all the eyes in the room have a great deal of respect for her.

Her health is visibly deteriorating by the minute. Her dress and hat are worn, but she continues to have an air of dignity as she searches the faces for resilience.

"Many years ago—more than I care to remember—my husband died. He was everything to me. He was my lover. He paid my bills, went to work, plowed a field, talked to people I didn't want to talk to, and on Saturday nights took his family out on the town to celebrate another week of living.

"When he died, I felt as though my world fell apart. You really don't know how important a person is until they're no longer there. I had to raise my children by myself, work and wear a mask almost every day of my life. I am so sick of the mask. Today I declare that I have retired the mask and you shall see who I really am.

"Today I am taking that mask off, and I am sharing my thoughts with you. Richard has promised us that his mask is coming off too. Sometimes masks are good, and sometimes a mask can slow down your growth. If I should die before the rest of you, I will need a spokesperson, too, to read this." She clears her throat as she starts to read:

Dear Fellow Journeymen,

I have completed years of travel. I have laughed some and cried some, but mostly laughed. I have fought for important issues in this life, which I thought would enhance others. I have stood my ground when the ground continued to move on me. There have been earthquakes, hurricanes, famines, and floods.

There have been rainbows, the sweet smell of rain and the ocean. There have been elegant mornings and evenings, with sprinkled love and sunshine along the way. And all along the way I've learned life is the best education anyone will ever get.

Now, this last assignment that the Creator gave me was the most challenging of all. What a sense of humor he had, placing me in a hostage situation where everyone had to learn to work together if anyone was going to get out alive.

Let me tell you what I learned from this last encounter. I learned that all children aren't on a course of self-destruction. I learned that just because someone is different from me that I don't have to shrink in my role as a person, and neither do they. I learned that if you're going to make any strides in life, you better know who you are. Know your family, know the people you call friends. Know the people you call your enemies, because all these people are important in the knowledge of self.

Whoever put us together knew what they were doing. Everyone in this room is totally different, and we spent the better part of our time working out our differences, but once those differences were settled, you should have seen us work together.

Finally, I believe that we have created a new fruit and vegetable with our ideas, which are relevant and important to the world. I do not want this work stifled for fear of stepping on someone's toes. The other captives and I will be true to the public, as well as being true to ourselves. If, for any reason, we fall away from that mark, we will ensure that someone in this group will help in bringing us back. Please do not let it come from our enemies.

We learned that we are killing nature, and once nature is gone, there is nothing else. No me and no you. All cameras should be centered on the United Nations as my fellow journeymen discuss the state of our Earth. I am proud that I was a part of this.

These are my thoughts, and I know that it is safe with this group of people who will soon be free because the lesson has already be learned, and the lesson that we learned is that if life is to work, we must work together.

Richard sits next to Mrs. McBride. "I will be the person who will read this when the time comes."

Chapter 29

"Hello," Rosa says after running to the phone.

"Well, hello, sweetie. Those were some moves you put on me last night. I'm ready for some more," Wilbert says in his sexiest voice.

"How can I help you?" Rosa says while trying to act professional.

"What do you mean 'How can I help you?' We got a deal, honey. I fulfilled my end of the deal. I got the FBI out of town, chasing down a lead in Atlanta. So don't you ask me how you can help me. I want you at the hotel tonight."

Rosa glances over at the people gathered around in the dining room going over evidence surrounding the kidnapping. There seems to be a breakthrough, and Rosa wants to be around to appear to be heroic and strong for her man Michael. Wilbert is crushing her plans, even though she has appreciation for him slowing down the process. The family seems to be getting closer to solving the mystery and getting Mrs. McBride back. Rosa is secretly annoyed that Mrs. McBride might be coming home soon, and being with Wilbert has cost her her pride.

"Sorry, I can't meet you tonight. The family needs me."

"What the hell are you talking about? I need you, and you better get your Black ass over to the hotel by seven o'clock or I'm going to tell yo' family just what you've been up to."

Wilbert hangs up the phone, and Rosa stands there looking down at it, deciding how she's going to tell Michael that she has to go out without him getting suspicious.

Precious watches Rosa and wonders where she is going at night and if she and Michael are getting back together. Rosa looks up and catches Precious staring at her. Rosa walks over to Michael, who is sitting at the dining room table. Rosa sits in his lap, angry at the idea that they might be getting close to finding Mrs. McBride.

"Please get up" is all Michael says to Rosa.

Mr. Lane says, "I believe that hillbilly you talked to yesterday. I don't believe that the Knights of Darkness have her. But what I can't figure out is who does and why do they have her?"

Michael stares at the sheets of paper that Jazzy has laid before him, and he doesn't speak for a while. When he does, he seems engrossed in the papers on the table. "My gut tells me that she's out in the fields of that farm somewhere. I can hear her call me from there. We can't get the local police to help. Kevin and I went to see Wilbert today, and we showed him all that I have. He's telling me that he believes she's in Atlanta. I say that we get Wendy's friends and anyone else who wants to help and go out into the forest. I believe that this is where we're going to find Mother."

Precious watches as Rosa strokes Michael's hair. Jazzy watches as Precious's attention has been diverted momentarily.

Wendy is sitting up straight as she says, "I'm ready tonight. Let's go."

"No," Michael says, still glaring at the pages in front of him. "We'll go early tomorrow morning, as soon as there's daylight, and I'm not stopping until I find her."

Mr. Lane says, "I'm with you. I've closed down the store, but I'll have my children bring food out to the site tomorrow until we find her."

Rosa stands up and walks over to where she left her purse. "I need some air. Anybody want anything from the store?"

Wendy can't believe her eyes. "You've taken off three times this week. Where are you going? You don't know anybody in town."

Rosa picks up her purse. She doesn't want attention focused on her, but now she can tell that everyone in the room is inquisitive. "Would you like to go with me, Wendy?"

"No, I wouldn't."

"So then why do you care where I go?"

"'Cause I know that you ain't up to any good. How is it you ain't scared to go out at night?"

"I know karate." Rosa smiles, picks up a cigarette, and walks out of the door. Angrily she starts up the car and heads toward Columbus to the hotel.

Michael is lying on the couch sleeping and wakes up staring at the grandfather clock in the living room. Finally he hears a car pull up in front of the mansion. He checks the clock one more time. It reads 5:00. He wipes the sleep away from his eyes as he gets up and moves toward the Gucci luggage sitting next to the door.

The door opens, and there stands Rosa, her hair hanging down in her face. Her dress is inside out, and she has one shoe on and is holding the other shoe in her hand. She is shocked to open the door and see Michael standing there.

"Good morning, love. Would you like some coffee?" Michael is quite chipper as he escorts Rosa into the house.

"Hi" is all she can manage to say. She tries to think of something fast. "I was out taking a walk. I forgot all about the time."

"Don't worry about that, my love. Step on into the house."

Rosa can sense that something is wrong, but she doesn't know what yet.

"Bertha told me that you weren't feeling well a couple of days ago."

"Yeah, but I'm feeling much better now."

"Is that right? I got a call from Roger, a friend of mine. He told me that he sent a man out here the other day to open up my mother's safe. Do you know anything about that?"

"Yeah. Since you were out looking for your mother, I wanted to make sure that the legal ends were all tied up."

"Tied up how?"

Rosa thinks for several seconds. "I wanted to make sure that if anything happened to your mother that you wouldn't have to fight about your share of the inheritance with your sister. You know Wendy is kinda crazy."

"Another question, my love. Why did you come here?"

"I came back to be by your side. I know how much you love your mother. I wanted to be here to have your back. That's why I did what I did the other day. I was looking out for your best interest."

"Is that why you were dancing around the room?"

"What are you talking about?"

"Bertha said when she got home with your prescription that you were dancing around the room. Is that correct?"

Rosa moves closer to Michael. "I wasn't dancing. I was exercising. I was trying to get my body going. I haven't exercised in a while."

"Is that right? I thought it was because you found my mother's bank statement in the safe."

"No, absolutely not. I didn't even find a bank statement."

"That is so weird, Rosa. When I was packing your luggage I found the bank statement in your bed."

"Packing my bags?" Rosa looks around the room. Michael steps aside, and she sees all her luggage packed up and ready to go.

"What's this?"

"Well, I thought about it. You weren't here when my father died. I couldn't even get you to take my calls. While I was here bathing him, taking care of the farm, I wondered where my woman was. You didn't even send my family a card. Now you show up going through my mother's personal items, taking charge of things you shouldn't be taking charge of, and never once did you ask me if there are any clues to her disappearance."

"But I was always here for you. It wasn't a rose garden living in California taking care of the responsibilities there while you were gone. Someone had to go to work and keep up the payments on that home that you bought."

"You could have called. You could have called and talked to my mother. I will never forget what you did. I called you and asked you to come to the funeral. My love, you didn't even call me back. Every time I look at you, I think about that. I'm not sure why you're back now. You didn't like my mother, and I'm not sure if you ever liked me either. I came from my mother. She's the one who taught me the ways of the world. If you don't like her, there's no way you're gonna ever love me. It took me some time to get to this place, but I want you out of here. You're only adding more confusion to my life."

"It's that woman, isn't it?"

"What woman?"

"That heifa that came down here from Michigan."

"She is not a cow, and no, it isn't her, but she opened my eyes. It took me three years, but I'm over you. I don't care where you were tonight, but I'll know where you will be tomorrow. Wendy will be taking you to the airport. Your plane leaves for California at seven o'clock, in a couple of hours. Wendy," Michael shouts upstairs.

Wendy is down the stairs in seconds.

"You were up there spying on us, weren't you?" Rosa is distraught as she confronts Wendy.

Wendy is fully dressed with another veil over her face. "What are you talking about? My brother asked me to take you to the airport."

"You're behind this whole thing." Rosa is tapping her foot, not knowing with whom she is angrier.

Michael and Wendy take the luggage outside. As the bags are placed into the truck, Michael has a second thought. "I'll take her to the airport, and you take her rental car back. I want to make sure she's on the plane."

Wendy says, "Deal" as she returns to the house.

Michael asks, "Where are you going?"

"I'm going to call a friend to meet me there."

Michael looks down at his Timex watch as he says, "You know as soon as I get back we're going to be looking for Mom."

Wendy is so happy to see Rosa leave, she says to Michael, "I'll be back in time. I've got about a hundred people who're going to meet us here."

"Good deal. I'll see you back here." Michael helps Rosa into the truck. As she yanks away from him, she almost falls over as she gets into the truck.

At seven o'clock about five hundred people gather in the driveway awaiting instructions. All the trucks and cars follow Michael as the mortician puts flags on everyone's vehicle.

Wendy asks, "Why are we putting those funeral flags on the cars?"

The mortician stares at Wendy for several seconds before saying, "Why are you living like you're already dead?"

"I'm concerned about my mother."

The mortician does not let her response stop him. "You've always dressed like you were dead. The funeral flags are to keep the cars together so that no one will get lost."

The mortician waves to several people as they get into their cars. The procession drives down the highway peacefully until they finally reach their destination and park. Walking in a straight line, they start into the wooded area. Just as they begin to walk, they hear sirens careening toward them.

Wilbert swaggers out of the police car with two cars trailing him. "What do y'all think you're doing?"

Michael steps out of the group and says, "I'm looking for my mother. I know that she's in these woods somewhere. I can't seem to get you to help us, so I'll help myself."

"Do you have these people's permission to be on their land?"

"Yep. We got permission yesterday."

"All this land doesn't belong to them. Some of the land belongs to the Indians. Did you get their permission?"

"No. I couldn't find the owners of the land."

"Well, until you do, I can't let you go destroying their land."

Wendy walks up to Wilbert. "Aren't you out of your jurisdiction?"

"My jurisdiction is anywhere I want to be, young lady."

"I don't think so. I think yours ended two counties ago."

Jazzy walks up behind Wendy. "You know, Wendy, I think you're right."

"Well, I'll just get the local police out here too."

Michael pushes past the two women as he says, "Go get the local police. In the meantime, I'll be looking for my mother."

Michael waves his hand to the group and once again they head into the forest.

Chapter 30

Richard and DeShan debate whose shoulders the rest of the captives should climb up on. The two of them have larger shoulders than the rest of the group. Finally Richard concedes and climbs up on DeShan's shoulders. Abu is lifted up next. The three of them wobble several seconds before they become steady enough for Nantan to climb up. Jessica is cheering the men as they try to hoist Nantan up past them. Nantan's shoe is in Abu's face before the group gives way and falls to the floor. Instead of crying because of a failed attempt or the pain it caused when they landed on the floor, the group starts laughing. They have a hearty laugh for several minutes.

Night is approaching without a trace of Mrs. McBride. Wilbert asks Michael what has happened to Rosa.

"I didn't know you knew my ex-wife."

"Yeah. The little lady came into the station asking me to help her find your mother. That little lady cares about your mother."

Michael is stunned; he knows that Rosa only cares about herself. "So did you help her?"

Wilbert tries to remain positive. "I've tried every way I could think of to help that young woman and you too."

"Is that why you sent the FBI to Atlanta?"

Wilbert whispers to Michael, "Well, you think you're awful smart, don't you?"

"Yeah, I am pretty smart. What did it cost my ex-wife to keep up this performance?"

Wilbert whispers, "What do you think it cost?"

"I have no idea, but I bet the FBI would like to know. They'll probably want to know who beat me up that day and who ran Precious out of the cottage that night too. I've got a lot to tell them about the police department in our town. As I see it, you've got a choice. You didn't try to find my mother, and it was left up to me to try to find her. All these men out here would whip your ass if I told them how you hindered this investigation and how you beat me up. You can either let me find my mother or you can get the kinda ass whippin' you gave me that day.

"You know how I know it was you, Wilbert? It was those shoes you have on. You've been wearing the same shoes for years. When I was on the ground I got a real good look at those ugly shoes.

"You see, Wilbert, you do have a choice."

Wilbert decides not to hinder the group and watches them as they head out into the woods. The search group continues to grow as word of the search party reaches other counties. There are around a thousand people out as Mr. Lane gives the group instructions. Mr. Lane, Precious, and Jazzy become Michael's and Wendy's strength as they continue the search.

DeShan, Richard, Abu, and Nantan try again and are about to reach the top of the room they are in, but they fall a fifth time. The crash and scream reach out into the forest as they nurse their injuries.

It is now seven o'clock in the evening, and the search party is about to call it off for the day when Precious and Jazzy scream out to the rest of the group that they heard something.

Searchers run over and look down on a sophisticated shelter dug into the ground. Car tracks lead out onto a dirt road, and soda and beer cans litter the area around the underground dwelling. Several men run back to their cars while others try to find an entrance to the dungeon. They find stairs that lead down to the dwelling.

At the bottom is a door. Michael tries to open the door. It's locked. He then beats on the door. "Is anyone in here?" Pounding sounds come from within.

"Please help us."

The door is heavy, and the men try to open it without success. Mr. Lane, who has a crowbar in his backpack, tries to pry the door open while others pull on the door. Slowly they are rewarded for their hard work as the door at last opens. They can't believe what they see.

There inside, amid the stench of filthy living conditions, are a small group looking toward the open door.

DeShan stands and asks, "Who are you?"

Michael smiles as he looks around the room for his mother and finds her lying on the floor. "We're here to rescue you."

"Mrs. McBride," DeShan shouts, "we've been rescued."

There is no response from Mrs. McBride. She lies motionless on the floor. There is a look of horror as someone shakes her. Still no answer.

DeShan picks her up and walks out of the door and up the stairs.

"I'll take her. She's my mother," Michael says, following DeShan up the stairs.

DeShan, who has gathered enough strength to carry Mrs. McBride, says, "No one touches her. Where is the car?"

Michael sees the determined expression on DeShan's face and makes a path for DeShan as he carries his friend out of the building.

At that moment, several cars race toward the group. Wilbert is following them. Michael points to Wilbert's car, and DeShan sprints toward the police car. "Come on, man. Get her to the hospital as fast as you can." Michael squeezes in the backseat with his mother and DeShan.

Several hours pass and hundreds of people are standing around in the hospital waiting room, in the hall, and outside. They are waiting for a doctor to tell them that Mrs. McBride is going to be all right. Precious is in disbelief that someone could just snatch your life away from you in a matter of minutes. How could this happen, and the police with all their sophisticated equipment could not find Mrs. McBride.

Jessica, Richard, Abu, and DeShan are talking together in the corner of the room. Jazzy whispers something to Jessica, then whispers the message to Precious. Both Jessica and Precious hug each other as Precious says to her, "I am so glad you are all right. I saw you that day on the highway in Michigan."

Mr. Lane and his son watch the drama from the center of the room.

Wilbert walks into the room with an older man wearing handcuffs straggling behind him.

"Who is that?" Jazzy asks others in the room.

Michael replies, "Why, that's David Eagle Feather. He lives on the reservation where they were holding everyone, where the underground prison was."

The people in the room gather around to listen to Wilbert. "You see, Mr. Eagle Feather here is responsible for the kidnapping. He thought that if he could get the greatest minds in the world together that they could change the world in some way. Just one thing he forgot. You can't go around kidnapping people. This man is going to jail for a long time. But he wanted me to bring him here first. Something he wants to say."

Richard walks over to the man who appears too old to spend any time in jail.

"I don't get it. Why did you do it?"

David Eagle Feather stands proud and says, "You offer us casinos and money to placate us while you destroy the lands my ancestors lived on. The Earth is headed for destruction. I took the money from the casinos and brought together some of the most brilliant minds to help solve this problem, and they did."

He looks at the captives. " Whenever you were able to work together, you received sunlight. When you were not able to work together, I turned off the sun. I never expected to keep you longer than two days. I thought you would be able to figure it out within a week. I forgot about the hatred you have for people who don't look like you. Had it not been for the hate, you would have solved the problem sooner."

DeShan walks over to him. "How come you just didn't ask us?"

"Because you all are too busy in your meaningless lives, and I knew you wouldn't come. A year ago I did ask you to come to this meeting. I asked all of you. I told you that I would pay for your stay, and each and every one of you turned me down. Too busy, you said."

Michael moves closer to him. "My mother is in critical condition because of what you did. She sat with you almost every morning, and you brought in the sun together, and you turned around and did this to her? I ought to kill you right now." Michael lunges toward him, and Wilbert holds Michael back.

Wendy walks into the room with Mrs. McBride's medications. She hasn't heard the confession and is wondering why Michael is being held.

"Hello, Mr. Eagle Feather," she says, approaching the group.

Wilbert scratches his head. "What do you know about this man?"

"He's Nantan's grandfather. Nantan and I attended the same grade school and high school together."

Everyone is staring at Nantan.

Jessica walks up to him. "You knew about this? You who were in the room with us, you knew about this?"

Nantan backs up. "Yes, I knew, but I didn't know that they were going to leave us, and I didn't mean for anything bad to happen to anyone, especially Mrs. McBride."

DeShan gives a sarcastic laugh. "So you were telling them what we were doing on the inside. How did you do it? I was watching you all the time."

"I did it with the chants. I knew when they were outside, and I told them how you were acting on the inside. You don't seem to understand the importance of this mission."

DeShan is angry. "And you don't seem to realize that you're responsible for the condition of Mrs. M. Who made you God to play with our lives like that? Even God gives us free will. You just plucked us out of our lives and put us in a situation that we will never recover from."

Dr. Smith walks into the room. "Wendy, did you get Mrs. McBride's medications?"

Wendy hands him the plastic bag with Mrs. McBride's prescriptions. Dr. Smith examines the bag. Dr. Smith is shocked. "Did any of you know that Mrs. McBride has a bad heart?" He whispers something to the nurse and takes off down the hallway toward Mrs. McBride's room.

Chapter 31

Several hours pass before Dr. Smith reenters the waiting room. "She wants to talk to the captives."

They walk into her room, not sure what to do. She is lying there helpless, and she says, "I'm not going to be able to complete the journey with you. Richard, I want you to represent me well. You will read my letter?"

Richard nods as he becomes stronger listening to her.

Mrs. McBride struggles to say, "I want to thank you for the experience we had together, and even though I won't be with you physically, I will be watching you."

She closes her eyes, and DeShan motions for everyone to leave the room. DeShan is the last person out, and he turns around, comes back into the room, and gives Mrs. McBride a hug and kisses. She smiles, but doesn't open her eyes.

Dr. Smith comes back out into the waiting area. "Mrs. McBride wants to talk with Michael, Wendy, Bertha, and David Eagle Feather. We are still trying to get her stabilized, so you have only three minutes."

Michael asks, "Is my mother going to be all right?"

Dr. Smith says, "I don't know."

Precious takes a seat in front of the television and looks at the picture, but her mind is on what is going on in the hospital room.

Michael, Wendy, Bertha, and David Eagle Feather walk back into the waiting room.

Michael walks over to Precious. "Mom wants to talk to you, Precious."

She can't believe it but she walks cautiously down the hall, knowing instinctively what room Mrs. McBride is in. Precious walks into the room and finds a once-proud woman lying helpless with a heart monitor next to the bed. She takes off the breathing mechanism as she motions for Precious to come closer to the bed.

"You wanted to know what heaven is like?"

Precious nods. Out of everything that has happened, she wonders how Mrs. McBride remembers that conversation so long ago.

"It is beautiful and I feel at peace in this place. Take care of Michael and Wendy for me?"

Precious's tears are flowing. "We'll take care of them together."

"Yeah, we will, but not like you think." This is all she says before she goes back to sleep. Precious places the breathing mechanism back on her face.

Precious stands for several minutes, digesting Mrs. McBride's words, before going back out into the waiting room.

An argument is ensuing as Precious approaches the group. Mrs. McBride has asked for clemency for David Eagle Feather, and Michael is having a difficult time forgiving him.

Wilbert walks over to Precious. "What did Mrs. McBride say to you?"

"It's personal."

Precious, who is having a difficult time understanding what is going on, says to Michael. "What happened?"

"Mom wants me to forgive him."

Wendy puts the veil over her face as she starts to cry.

Michael puts his arm around his sister and says, "I can't forgive him."

Dr. Smith walks back into the room. "I'm sorry."

"You're sorry? Why are you sorry?" Michael asks, fretful.

"Your mother has just expired."

A quiet storm hovers around the room.

Dr. Smith continues, "Your mother never told anyone that she had heart problems. She told me after I challenged her about the pills. You know what she told me? She told me that she was given no more than two months to live anyway. I had my nurse call her doctor, and he confirmed that. She told me that the work that she just completed with the Black farmers and the captives was the most important work that she has ever done in her life, except for raising her children."

Michael turns to the group who were in confinement together and asks, "What work?"

DeShan, who is about to whimper, says, "We can get together later, and I'll fill you in." DeShan turns to the captives, and asks, "Where's the letter Mrs. M. wrote?"

Jessica hands DeShan the letter. DeShan holds it as if it is made of gold. He hands it to Richard. "This is your assignment. Please don't mess it up."

Chapter 32

There is standing room only as hundreds of people are trying to speak at Mrs. McBride's home-going. The minister finally calls a halt to speakers and calls Richard up to speak. Richard is powerful as he reads the letter Mrs. McBride left.

Wendy has on a stunning blue hat and a suit that accentuates her beautiful skin tone. This is the first time anyone has seen Wendy dressed in normal attire. When Michael asks her why, she says, "I have to become the woman that my mother was. I'm going to represent her and take up the leadership banner. I'm going to complete the master's program in agricultural science and I'm coming back to take up the cause for the Black farmers."

Afterward, the captives and Precious, Jazzy, and close family members gather in Mrs. McBride's living room, and the meeting begins.

Mr. Lane and Kevin, the detective from Michigan, are in the corner of the room discussing an important issue, and they become animated as they talk.

Jessica holds up her finished work. "I've got the report finished," she says proudly to the group.

"Okay," Michael says, finally understanding the importance of the project. "Abu has gotten us on the agenda with the United Nations next month. We need spokespeople. Who would you suggest?"

Jessica rises and says, "That's already been taken care of, and Mrs. McBride gave her blessing to DeShan and Nantan for this audacious assignment."

Nantan is sitting there waiting for someone to say he cannot be the spokesman.

Finally, Richard says it. "I don't think he should represent us. He stabbed us in the back. Mrs. McBride would have been alive today if it hadn't been for Nantan. He could have told them to open the door for her, but he didn't. How come he isn't in jail?"

Nantan defends himself. "I did tell them to open the door, but they were gone, and we were truly alone. I wasn't arrested. I didn't know she was going to die, and I didn't know that they were going to leave us. I'm going to testify against my family. That should show you how serious I am about this. Those gunmen were relatives. I will never be able to go back to my tribe again after this. Never."

Jessica brings the Bible over to him and puts his hand on the cover. "You have told the whole truth and nothing but the truth?"

"I have."

DeShan says to everyone. "He could have left, but he didn't. He suffered just like the rest of us. I say we give him a chance. Most of the information for the report came from Nantan anyway."

Wendy says in the tone of voice Mrs. McBride would have used, "He will stay in the group. He was part of the group, and my mother has said that he should represent the group at the United Nations, and as far as I'm concerned, that's good enough for me. I have known Nantan all my life, and there's no one more concerned about life than he is. He stays in the group, and he speaks when the time comes." The hat on Wendy's head is worn like the hat Mrs. McBride wore, and everyone is silent for several seconds, looking at Wendy and the spirit of Mrs. McBride in her.

Abu says in an uneven voice, "I agree. He should speak."

DeShan is nervous. "I think someone else should present this information to the United Nations other than myself."

Jessica asks, not caring what his answer will be, "So you're going to let Mrs. McBride down because you're scared? We all are scared. I know you can do it."

Michael puts his arm around him, and says, "Man, you can do this."

DeShan breathes hard one last time and says, "I'm doing this one for Mrs. M."

A car pulls up in front of the mansion and two men get out. They look as if they are from the FBI. They waste no time getting to the point of their visit. "David Eagle Feather is going to jail for the rest of his life."

Michael walks over toward the men. "My mother has known Mr. Eagle Feather for over thirty years. She asked that he be allowed to go free."

The other captives agree, but this seems to fall on deaf ears.

The first agent, who appears to outrank the other agent standing beside him, says, "We are glad that you are so forgiving, but it's against the law to take people away against their will. We had FBI agents looking for you, and it has cost the agency a lot of money. So he is going to jail for a long time."

The agent goes on to say, "What were you working on while you were locked away?"

DeShan walks over and stands next to Michael. "We were discussing how important it is for us to be together at this period of time in life."

The first agent in his white short-sleeve shirt and black pants turns to Nantan. "Will you testify about what was going on?"

"Not much to testify to. We were hostages, couldn't get out, and finally someone other than you came to get us out."

No one says a word. The FBI agents go back out to their car and sit for several minutes. Wendy notices that they're making phone calls.

Several minutes later, two trucks and five more cars pull up in front of the mansion. The two men walk back into the house and say, "We are confiscating all the computers and papers related to this case." They snatch the reports out of Jessica's hand.

Jazzy asks, "Why?"

"We've deemed that what you were doing in the dungeon is a general safety measures hazard, and the powers want to know what was going on."

Jessica is guarded as she says, "We plan to tell them what we talked about. What we discussed is a win-win situation for everyone. We're trying to help you."

"Yeah, sure you are." He turns and tells several men, "Take all the computers to the truck."

The computers are piled into the truck. Jazzy, Jessica, and Precious walk out onto the porch as the vehicles maneuver down the road. All three women wave good-bye to the group as they disappear out of sight.

Michael cannot believe his eyes. "What are you three doing? They took everything we have. We have nothing to present to the United Nations now."

Jessica smiles. "Jazzy has a computer in her purse. We downloaded everything into her computer. You see, this happened to me before in Michigan, and I wasn't going to make that same mistake again."

They all laugh as they think about how Mrs. McBride would be so proud of them.

Mr. Lane and Kevin stand in the middle of the living room. Mr. Lane puts his arm around Kevin and says, "We have an announcement to make."

Everyone gathers around the men to find out what they have to say.

"I have decided to run for the mayor of this fine city this November," Mr. Lane says. "I'm doing this to honor the legacy of Mrs. McBride. I believe that we can make this town the town that it should be. I need to canvass the town for signatures, but I know that this isn't going to be a problem.

"Guess who will be running for the local sheriff of this fine city? Kevin told me that he would love to come down and help us out here, especially with the Knights of Darkness. He will have just made the residency rule, and I like the way this young man thinks."

Mr. Lane smiles as he adds, "Even though he and I will be busy until the election, we'll be in New York to support you."

Kevin smiles and says, "I've talked with the FBI, and they've promised to help me clean up the city. I can't wait to get started."

The room explodes into clapping and laughter as they congratulate both men on their decision to run for offices in the small town.

Finally, it is time for Precious and Jazzy to leave. They have their luggage in the car and are ready to say good-bye. Michael gives Jazzy a hug as she gets into the driver's seat. "Jazzy, I'm so glad you came down. If it hadn't been for you, I wouldn't have had a chance to say good-bye to my mother. Thank you so much for bringing your skills here."

Michael walks around to the passenger side of the car with Precious. "I'll see you in New York at the United Nations meeting next month?"

"Yep. I'll be there."

Michael pulls his pants up proudly and says, "I'm going to find an attorney for Mr. Eagle Feather only 'cause I told Mom I would do that. By the way, what did my mother say to you?"

Precious thinks fast. "She said heaven was a beautiful place."

"Precious?"

"Yes?"

"Will you marry me?"

Jazzy says, "Yes, she'll marry you."

"No, I didn't say that. Communication is a big deal for me. Let's see if we have conversations before the UN meeting."

Michael closes the car door after she carefully gets inside. He smiles and says, "Is that a yes?"

"Bye, Cowboy. I'll see you later."

Jazzy and Precious pull off down the dirt road, feeling a lot better about life. They both feel as though they've been carrying mountains on their backs for over a month. The mountains are gone and their lives are freer.

Several minutes later, Precious's phone rings. She picks it up, and Michael is on the other end of the line.

He says, "How about this for communicating? I miss you already."

Precious laughs. "You know I miss you too. I don't have anyone to fight with."

"Well, I'll talk to you soon then." Michael hangs up the phone.

Precious is about to board the plane when she receives another phone call. "Am I calling you too much?" It's Michael again.

"Pace yourself. How about talking once a day?"

"No, I can't do that. We'll talk three times a day—morning, noon, and night."

The plane takes off down the runway. Precious turns to Jazzy and says, "This is it. It's time to live."

It's the journey that counts.

The Beginning

LaVergne, TN USA
02 August 2010
191733LV00005B/33/A